UNIDENTIFIED

TREASURE HUNTER SECURITY #7

ANNA HACKETT

A NOVELLA DUO

Unidentified

Published by Anna Hackett

Copyright 2018 by Anna Hackett

Cover by Melody Simmons of eBookindiecovers

Edits by Tanya Saari

ISBN (ebook): 978-1-925539-49-3

ISBN (paperback): 978-1-925539-50-9

Unexplored – Romantic Book of the Year
(Ruby) Novella Winner 2017

At Star's End – One of Library Journal's Best
E-Original Romances for 2014

Return to Dark Earth – One of Library
Journal's Best E-Original Books for 2015 and
two-time SFR Galaxy Awards winner

The Phoenix Adventures – SFR Galaxy Award
Winner for Most Fun New Series and "Why
Isn't This a Movie?" Series

Beneath a Trojan Moon – SFR Galaxy Award
Winner and RWAus Ella Award Winner

Hell Squad – Amazon Bestselling Science Fiction Romance Series and SFR Galaxy Award for best Post-Apocalypse for Readers who don't like Post-Apocalypse

The Anomaly Series – #1 Amazon Action Adventure Romance Bestseller

Sign up for my VIP mailing list and get your *free box set* containing three action-packed romances.

Visit here to get started:
www.annahackettbooks.com

THE EMERALD TEAR

Anna Hackett

CHAPTER ONE

H is boots made a satisfying squelching sound in the mud as he crossed the jungle dig site.

Oliver Ward grinned. His mom would be horrified. She rarely stepped a designer-clad foot off the Denver sidewalk, if she could help it. His dad would have a manly, resigned look on his face, and Oliver's brother, Isaac, would just roll his eyes.

It didn't matter, though. Oliver couldn't be happier.

He was thirty-one years old and living his dream.

He scanned the dig site. Several of his team members from the University of Denver were with him, including his mentor, Ben McBride. The archeologist had taught Oliver everything he knew. One day, Ben would retire, and Oliver planned to take over from him. Professor Oliver Ward. It had a nice ring to it.

His gaze took in the irregularly-shaped cut stones embedded in the side of the muddy hill. They'd pushed the jungle back to give them access to the remnants of the stone works that had been previously lost to time. Unidentified ruins waiting for Oliver's team to discover their secrets and their place in history.

Archeology in Ecuador was improving, but even now, in the late seventies, it was still haphazard and disjointed from a lack of funding. He looked up at the thick jungle surrounding the site. Through the vegetation, he caught a glimpse of the river not too far down the hill.

It didn't help that the site was in the Amazon jungle, on the wild eastern side of Ecuador. His boots sank into the mud again. The wild terrain made everything harder.

There was a lot more archeology work going on in neighboring Peru—at the famous Inca ruins there. But Oliver knew there were fascinating Inca sites here, too, waiting to be discovered.

Just ahead, crouched down by the ruins of a rock wall, he saw Carlos Lopez, the local archeologist who'd brought in Oliver's team. The man was smart, and keen to improve the methods and understanding of both the pre-Incan and Incan cultures. He wanted to share the history of his country with the world.

"Oliver." A woman's voice made him turn.

"What have you got, Cheryl?" He crouched down beside the hole she was digging.

Dr. Cheryl Wilson was a good archeologist, although she didn't love fieldwork, and mostly enjoyed being inside the university lecture halls. She didn't hide her dislike of the mud, bugs, and the humidity. Still, he couldn't fault her dedication.

Cheryl lifted a shard of ceramic. He took it carefully,

studying it. Perhaps a piece of cooking pot. Cheryl was watching him, her gaze on his face. He stifled a sigh. She'd kept dropping hints about them having dinner or catching a show. She was a smart, attractive woman. She'd started the day with her blonde hair styled into feathered locks that swept away from her face. He'd seen the style become popular with the students at the university as well. But here, the heat and humidity of the jungle had left her curls somewhat bedraggled.

Back in Denver, Cheryl was the kind of woman he usually dated. But now, he felt...nothing but mild appreciation. To be fair, lately he'd been feeling disillusioned with dating. He gave in to the urge and heaved an internal sigh. No matter how attractive the women, he'd felt a lack of passion, excitement, and challenge.

Growing up, Oliver's father had wanted Oliver to follow in his footsteps and become a lawyer. Law had made Oliver feel the same way as his recent dates—bored and stifled.

History on the other hand... Excitement flooded his veins. The thrill of discovery, of uncovering parts of the past and fitting them together, making sense of where they'd come from, that's what lit Oliver on fire.

"Oliver?"

He blinked and saw Cheryl beaming at him. She probably thought his look was for her.

Shit. "Let's see." He lifted the pottery to eye level. "Doesn't look decorative. It's everyday stuff. This has to be a village." He scanned the structures. He was sure they had once been houses.

"You still think it's Inca?" she asked.

He nodded. "Probably." But what were they doing here in the dense jungle?

With a nod at Cheryl, he carried the ceramic shard over to the tent they'd set up to store their finds. Plastic tubs were filled with ceramic and carved stones. They had also found a couple of pieces of delicate gold jewelry.

Ben was working nearby. The older man raised a hand before bending back to his work. Pausing, Oliver set his hands on the hips of his mud-splattered cargo pants and studied the rest of the dig site. A couple of people were working higher up on the slope. He carefully traversed the slippery stones pressed into the mud and headed in their direction. He wondered why the people who'd built this place had placed these stones here, had built their homes here. What was so special about this spot?

"Hey, Oliver," Dr. Sam Fields, a close friend of Oliver's, called out. They'd studied together at college and been on several digs together.

"How's it going?" Oliver asked.

Sam winked. "Slow and dirty."

"I like it slow and dirty, dude," Cory Kowalski, another member of the team, said. The young man was a graduate student and they happily gave him all the dirty jobs.

Oliver smiled, then glanced upward. The sky filled with heavy, gray clouds. They'd get a downpour soon.

Suddenly, he heard a scream, followed by several shouts.

He spun and saw Cory sliding down the slope. The young man's arms were flailing, but as his boots slipped off the stone, they hit dirt and he slid faster.

Shit. Oliver leaped forward, his gaze shifting down to the long sweep of the Rio Napo. If Cory didn't stop, he'd end up going over the edge and into the caiman-infested water. No one wanted to find themselves face to face with the aggressive alligator-like predators.

Oliver reacted without thinking. He crouched, snatching up a coil of rope off a pile of gear near the edge of the dig. He ran across the slippery stones, praying he didn't slip, and then threw one end of the rope.

It snaked around a nearby tree. "Tie it off," he yelled.

Then he hurried down the slope after Cory. His boots skidded and more mud splattered up his khaki trousers.

Right near the steep edge of the river, Cory had managed to grab on to some tree roots, and was holding tight, his face lined with fear. Mud streaked his cheek.

Oliver pulled tight on the rope, coming to a stop just above the man. "Hang on, Cory."

The young man looked up and swallowed, his Adam's apple bobbing.

"I've got you." Oliver grabbed the man's arm and pulled him up.

Down by the river, Oliver heard a splash. He turned his head and saw that an interested caiman had slid off the bank.

No snack today, buddy.

Oliver quickly and expertly tied the rope around

Cory. The young man's chest was heaving. Looking back up the slope, Oliver waved at the others.

"We're going to take it nice and easy, and take our time walking back, okay?"

Cory nodded. Using the rope, they carefully navigated their way up the muddy slope. It was slow going, but finally they reached the others.

The young man collapsed on the ground. "You are one cool cat, Dr. Ward." He scraped a shaky hand over his face.

"You're welcome." Oliver slapped Cory on the back.

As Cheryl whisked Cory off, Oliver leaned over and pressed his hands to his thighs. His heart was still pumping hard and he took a second to catch his breath.

When he lifted his head, movement at the far edge of the dig, near the tree line, caught his eye. He spotted a small figure standing in the dense vegetation, sticking to the shadows.

Was it a local? He frowned. At that moment, the first few spots of rain splattered down, hitting his shoulders and arms.

From what he could make out, the person was small and slim, and wearing cargo pants and a khaki shirt. They had a hat pulled low over their face, but Oliver was sure the person was staring at him.

For some reason, his heart kicked against his ribs, then he watched as the figure turned and moved along the tree line with a quick, economic gait.

Then the heavens opened up and rain saturated Oliver's clothes.

Within seconds, he could barely see the trees, let alone the lone figure. He kept frowning. From the way the person moved, he was sure it was a woman.

Who was she? Why was she watching his dig?

Ben called out his name then, and with one final glance at the shadows, he turned to join the others.

PERSEPHONE BLAKE STRODE down the street in the provincial capital of Tena, Ecuador. Perched on the confluence of two rivers, the town was a regional hub, and the number of tourists visiting was growing—lured by intrepid adventures into the Amazon. They had several cheap hotels and hostels, including the best one, where the American archeologists were currently staying.

She nodded at a group of smiling kids playing with some dogs in the street. They grinned back at her, teeth white against their bronze skin and dark hair.

Reaching the doorway to a bar and restaurant, she yanked open the door and walked inside. It was a dive, but had a certain charm to it.

God, how many days had she spent like this in her twenty-six years? Walking into seedy bars or pubs? She'd lost count.

Persephone headed straight for the bar and ordered a tequila in Spanish.

Her Spanish was pretty good, her French passable, and her Portuguese a bit spotty. It was thanks to her good ol' dad that she could speak a smattering of half-a-dozen languages. He'd certainly dragged her around enough countries during her childhood.

The bartender nudged her drink toward her in a chipped glass of dubious cleanliness. She set the coins down on the scarred, wooden bar and took a mouthful of her drink. It was watered down, but it would do.

She'd spent most of her formative years in South and Central America, while her dad had worked mining, or oil and gas jobs. Her mother had popped into their lives whenever the hell it had suited her. Athena Blake only did things that suited her.

Persephone shoved all thoughts of her mother away and took another sip of her bad drink. She turned slightly, so she could see the group sitting at the back of the bar.

The archeologists had all showered and changed. She heard a higher-pitched laugh and zeroed in on the lone woman in the group. She was perched on the edge of her chair, wearing pants that were outrageously wide at the bottom, and had her blonde hair styled in huge feathered waves.

Persephone snorted. In less than an hour, the humidity in this country would make it a waste of time to do all that work on her hair. Persephone kept her own brown hair clipped short in a pixie cut. It was less hassle that way and required no styling. The group looked to be in good spirits, and Persephone saw the woman desperately trying to capture the eye of the man sitting beside her.

Couldn't blame the woman. The man was outrageously good-looking. Put him in a tuxedo and he'd make an excellent James Bond. He had thick, dark hair and an easy, sexy smile.

Even from a distance, Persephone felt a curl of heat lick her belly.

She squelched it. She had no time for men. They always disappointed her, no matter how pretty they looked. Besides, he'd spotted her today at the dig site. She must be losing her touch.

Setting her glass down, she reached inside her shirt and pulled out the papers she kept in a clear, waterproof sleeve.

The first thing she saw was a picture of a tropical island. White-sand beaches surrounded by azure waters. Her retirement goal.

The next thing she pulled out was a photocopy of a page out of a handwritten diary. The writing was loopy and hard to read.

This was key to her achieving her retirement plan.

Her plan was to be retired at thirty-five. Persephone wanted to be sunning herself on the beach and banging sexy surfers or fishermen. She stroked the copy of the diary page. It held clues from a 1920's expedition to find a fabulous treasure right here in Ecuador.

That group had been consumed by the jungle, but Persephone wasn't going to let that happen to her. She was made of tougher stuff.

She folded the island picture and another tattered picture fell out of the sleeve.

This one was of a lovely Victorian house, somewhere in the USA. She'd never seen the house in real life before. While she'd been born in the States, she hadn't spent a lot of time there. But she'd seen this picture in a magazine once, and something about it had captured her interest. It looked like the kind of house a tight-knit family lived in. A family who celebrated Christmas, Thanksgiving, and Fourth of July. She snorted. Persephone had never had a home, so she didn't know much about them.

She shook her head. It was silly that she'd kept the picture. She should throw it out. She was destined for a beach shack by white sand and blue waters.

She lifted the diary page. Right now, she needed to stay focused on following the clues, and solving her big problem—the fact that the archeology team were digging on the location of her first clue.

Oh, and she couldn't forget her other problem. The fact that Sosa, the asshole dealer who'd sold her the page, had also sold a copy to someone else. Which meant Persephone would likely have company of the not-so-friendly kind before too long.

When the treasure was an invaluable lost emerald of the Inca, it guaranteed problems.

Someone sat on the stool beside her, reeking of cheap whiskey.

"*Hola, bella,*" the man drawled.

She rolled her eyes and gave the man an Arctic glare.

Clearly, he was too drunk to read her signals. He set a beefy hand on her shoulder.

She shrugged him off. "Shove off," she said, in Spanish.

His face hardened. "Just want to have some fun."

"Not interested."

His thick brows pulled together. "You aren't being very friendly."

Great. She could deal with this buffoon, but it would attract unwanted attention.

"The lady said she wasn't interested."

The smooth voice spoke in perfect, accentless Spanish. She felt warmth along her spine as a firm body pressed close to her back. Every single one of her nerves flared to life.

"Piss off, *gringo*," the drunk muttered.

Persephone was done. She moved her foot, catching the leg of the stool. It tipped over, and the man sprawled on the floor with a string of curses.

The bartender leaned over the bar, barking out some rapid words to the man. The drunk glared at the bartender, then at Persephone, before he hauled himself to his feet. He unsteadily weaved his way to the door, ranting to nobody.

Persephone grabbed her drink and downed the last of her shot before she turned.

Mr. Mouthwatering Archeologist was even more handsome up close.

She discovered that he had beautiful, cobalt-blue eyes, and he smelled good. *Damn.*

"Nice move," he said with a smile.

"I didn't need a rescue." She slammed her glass back on the bar.

"I can see that." He tilted his head to the side. "Can I get you another drink?"

"Hell, no."

His sexy smile just widened. "Not the usual response I get when I offer to buy a woman a drink."

She snorted. "I bet." Persephone was sure that women fell over themselves whenever this man gave them any attention. Pretty, normal women, who wanted to play house with him, cook his meals, roll around naked in his bed, and give him pretty, well-behaved kids.

"I have to leave," she said.

"I wish you'd stay." His blue eyes bored into hers, like she was an interesting story that he couldn't wait to hear.

Staring at that gorgeous face muddled her brain. He was too handsome, too everything. Dammit, she never let anything or anyone fog up her head.

"Why?" She mentally cursed herself for opening her mouth.

He leaned closer. "Because I'd like to know why you were spying on my dig today."

Shit. She stiffened. God save her from smart men.

Persephone spun and strode toward the door. The man grabbed her arm and pulled her back.

Quick as lightning, she let her switchblade fall down her sleeve and into her palm. She flicked it open and out of view of everyone in the bar, she pressed it against his collarbone.

"I don't like being grabbed."

He lifted his hands, palms up. "Fair enough." His voice lowered. "But I will admit I liked touching you."

Persephone wasn't dumb. She felt the electric current arcing between them. *Dammit.* He was a complication she didn't need.

"Forget you saw me," she said.

"Never going to happen." Again, she got that sexy smile.

Because she felt her brain fogging up again, she pressed her blade a little harder against his skin. He jerked back, and a thin line of blood welled.

Persephone used the distraction to spin under his arm and escape out of the bar.

CHAPTER TWO

Early the next morning, Oliver pulled on a fresh set of clothes. He knew he should be focused on the work he had to get done at the dig, but instead, he was thinking of his feisty mystery woman from the night before.

He rubbed the small cut on his collarbone and smiled. He was pretty sure she would've stabbed him, if he'd given her a good enough reason.

His smile widened. Maybe not. He'd seen interest in her eyes. Reluctant, but it was there.

She'd been a pint-sized package. Five feet tall if she was lucky, with brown hair cut short to follow the shape of her head. She had big, gray eyes, and a chip a mile wide on her shoulder.

A fist thumped on his door. "We're ready to go, Oliver." Ben's muffled voice.

"Coming." Oliver tucked his shirt into his work trousers. He had work to do. Grabbing his backpack off the rickety bed, he headed for the door. The hotel where they were staying was far from fancy, but the simple, tiled rooms were clean, and did the job.

Outside, a lush, little garden filled the small space. Across the road from the hotel, he saw the slow slide of the river. It passed through the town of Tena, and later met up with the larger Rio Napo.

But even as he moved toward his team, who were waiting by the battered Jeeps, he wondered if he'd see the woman again.

"Who's ready to get muddy?" Oliver called out.

There was a chorus of laughs and groans.

He rode in the passenger seat beside Ben. The others were all chatting about the work they had planned for the day.

When they reached the mud-splattered site, Oliver felt a sense of rightness. He smiled and got right to work.

Soon, he was hot and sweaty, and his hands were coated in mud. Cory was working beside him, carefully pulling artifacts out of the dirt.

"Those stones covering the hill, they have to mean something," the young man said.

Oliver grunted. He'd learned not to make judgments without all the information he could glean. But he had to admit, there were some strange, unique carvings on the stones. They were all images of boats, and they all pointed toward the river. It had to mean something.

"I think it has to be something important. Maybe even the Tomb of Atahualpa." Cory's voice was laced with awe. "That would be so ace."

Oliver shook his head. He remembered being a

student, heading off on hard, dusty digs, hoping to discover a lost temple or tomb. Over the years, he'd learned that the little things were just as important. A carved-bone toy a child had once held, the shard of a pot that people had used to cook with, a piece of jewelry a man had once given the woman he loved. Archeology wasn't always about the grand discoveries, and the bread and butter were the small things.

"It's definitely an Inca site," Oliver said. "But I don't think it's grand enough for the tomb of an emperor. It looks like these were homes of ordinary people." And Oliver didn't care if they were kings or workers. It was still a mystery for him to solve.

Cory looked disappointed.

Oliver clapped the younger man's shoulder. "This is important, too. This kind of work is the foundation. Each piece we discover is a part of the puzzle. It might not be glamorous, but you're doing good work here."

Cory's gaze brightened and he nodded.

Oliver looked out at the thick jungle surrounding them. "Well, one thing we know is that they probably weren't farmers."

"Fishermen?"

"Maybe." Although he'd seen no evidence of that, yet.

Oliver fell back into his work, completely unfazed by the mud on his clothes. But one part of his brain was still thinking about his mystery woman. All of a sudden, he heard startled shouts, followed by the sharp *rat-a-tat-tat* of gunfire.

He instantly dropped to the ground. "Get down," he roared.

A group of bandits was coming down the slope, all wearing dark-green fatigues. They looked like locals. They already had several of his team members rounded up, prodding them forward with their AK-47s.

Fuck. Oliver jumped to his feet. "What's going on—?"

The closest bandit turned, ramming the butt of his weapon into Oliver's gut. He hunched over, air rushing out of him. Damn, that hurt.

Beside him, he saw the men were forcing his archeologists onto their knees. Carlos started speaking in Spanish, but one of the bandits barked at him, and he fell silent. The bandits started ransacking the artifact tent and their gear. Bins of pottery were upended on the ground, and Cheryl cried out.

Oliver gritted his teeth. There was no treasure here, nothing of monetary value. What the hell were they possibly looking for?

He glanced up and saw that a trio of bandits were standing near the stonework covering the hill. One was crouched, studying something. Oliver frowned. The three men were gesticulating and talking among themselves. It looked like they were looking for something specific.

There was more crashing as the other men tore through the artifact tent. He watched one take out a large knife and started slicing at the canvas. Anger burned through Oliver's veins. Ransacking was one thing, but this was just willful destruction.

The trio by the hill called out and the bandits pulled back. Most of them disappeared into the trees. But two stayed close by, picking through the remnants of the artifacts.

"You won't get away with this," Ben called out.

The closest bandit moved over and smacked the older man in the face. Ben grunted in pain and grabbed his cheek. Then the bandit lifted his fist to hit Ben again.

Oliver lunged and caught the man's hand before it made contact. Their gazes locked, and Oliver stared him down. He wasn't going to stand there and let his friend get hurt. The bandit sneered, and as he yanked on his hand, Oliver pulled back a fist and punched the man in the face.

With a grunt, the bandit staggered backward. At that moment, the second bandit stepped in between them. He lifted his rifle and aimed it straight at Oliver's face.

Oliver froze. *Fuck.* He heard Cheryl crying, and the others calling out.

Breathless moments passed, and then the sound of a gunshot echoed through the trees.

Oliver flinched, but after a second, he realized that nothing had hit him. He wasn't dead or riddled with bullets.

Right in front of him, the man holding the gun stumbled to his knees. Blood bloomed on his shoulder, soaking his shirt.

Oliver crouched and spun. *What the hell was going on?* His boot slipped on the slick mud, but he managed to stay on his feet.

A small figure sauntered out of the trees, hat sitting low on their head and a handgun clutched in their hands.

It was her!

Oliver watched the woman march closer. She reached them, barked something in Spanish to the bandit, then kicked him in the chest.

He fell to the ground and the other bandit moved. The woman turned her gun, training it on the man. He went still.

"I think you saved my life," Oliver said.

Gray eyes whipped up to his. "Guess you owe me, then."

He smiled. "I'm actually not too cut up about that."

Cheryl made a sound. "Oliver, do you *know* this woman?"

He didn't take his eyes off his savior.

But just then, the injured bandit leaped upward. He slammed into the woman.

Oliver saw her eyes widen, then she was tumbling down the slippery slope with the bandit.

"No!" Without thinking, Oliver dove after her.

PERSEPHONE WAS FALLING. *Shit.*

Great. Just great. She bumped over the ground, sliding through the mud. Below, she caught a glimpse of the sunlight glinting off the river.

She tried desperately to stop her fall, but she seemed to be picking up speed, mud flying around her.

Before she could come up with any ideas, she hit the water with a splash.

She looked up, and saw the asshole she'd shot struggling wildly in the water. It didn't look like he could swim.

The bastard's panicked eyes locked on her and he grabbed her. *Dammit.* He dragged her under with him, and her mouth filled with water. She kicked at him, trying to get him off her.

She came up for air, vaguely aware of hearing another splash nearby. *Don't be a caiman. Don't be a caiman.*

A second later, Dr. Handsome was there, tearing the man off her. He pushed the man away, grabbed a fistful of her shirt, and then kicked strongly toward the riverbank.

As they swam, Persephone saw several caimans pop up out of the water nearby. *Dammit.*

"Ward," she snapped.

He lifted his head and saw the beasts. He pulled her closer and kicked harder. She kicked as well, trying to help.

They reached the steep bank and both of them grabbed handfuls of the thick, green plants. She tried to pull herself up, but the mud was so slick that she kept slipping back. She cursed loudly and enthusiastically.

She heaved again, but this time, firm hands gripped her hips and pushed her out of the water. For a brief moment, she felt Oliver Ward's face pressed against her butt. Then he tossed her up on to the bank. She grabbed some vines and held on tight before glancing back.

The bandit's screams cut through the air. She saw thrashing coming from the river, and her stomach curdled. More caimans were converging, and she knew the blood in the water would also draw the piranhas.

And Ward was still in the river.

She reached down with one hand and gripped the neck of his shirt.

"Move higher," he growled. "Get to safety."

She ignored him, and tugged and pulled. He muttered a curse, got his boots up onto the muddy bank, and together, they pulled him out of the water. He landed beside her, and then they climbed up the bank to flatter ground.

"Shit." She face-planted onto the dirt, chest heaving.

"Hell." He flopped onto his back beside her, eyes closed.

"Quite a morning, Ward," she said.

He turned his head and opened his eyes. Their faces were only inches apart.

"You know my name."

She'd made it her business to find out who he was after the bar. Dr. Oliver Ward—smart, ambitious archeologist from the University of Denver. He was staring at her, and then he reached out and cupped her jaw, the look on his face intense.

Persephone knew it was coming and she did nothing to avoid it. The next thing she knew, his mouth pressed against hers.

Damn. His lips were firm but had just the right amount of give. His tongue slid into her mouth and she tasted him. Instantly, she fell into the sexy fog this man seemed to induce in her, and she kissed him back.

Her tongue tangled with his, her hand sliding into his thick hair. He groaned, deepening the kiss, and she bit his lip. God, she wanted to eat him up.

Somewhere above them, she heard voices.

They pulled apart, both of them panting.

"I'm Oliver Ward," he said.

"I know."

He sank a hand into her wet hair. "Tell me your name."

She didn't answer, and he kept staring at her.

"I want to know," he murmured quietly. "Please."

Damn him. "Persephone. Persephone Blake."

Gently, almost delicately, he tucked her hair behind her ear, and her heart spasmed. It was stupid. They were both wet and covered in mud.

"Hi, Persephone," he murmured.

Time to go. She tried to get up.

"No." His hold on her tightened. "I want to know what the hell is going on. Who are you?"

"Your worst nightmare."

"I doubt that." A small smile flirted on his lips. "Although, I will confess that you did star in some of my dreams last night."

A wicked curl of heat hit her belly. "I'm someone that you have *nothing* in common with."

"I beg to differ."

She snorted. "You're an upstanding archeologist." She smiled thinly. "I'm a treasure hunter."

Persephone had expected a reaction, but the damn man just raised a brow.

"So, we both like history."

She shook her head.

"And we don't mind getting a bit dirty to get the job done."

A surprised laugh burst out of her. "You're crazy."

He rubbed her cheek with his thumb. "I need you to tell me why everyone is suddenly so interested in my dig."

She shook her head.

"Tell me."

"No."

"I can help you."

"I work alone."

"Not anymore," he said darkly.

"Ward—"

Suddenly, he moved fast, and she let out a squeak. She felt something settle on her wrist and looked down. She sucked in a breath. He'd tied her wrist to his with a short length of rope she'd seen on his belt.

Her mouth dropped open. "You into kink, Ward?"

She got a brain-fogging, sexy smile as a reply. "No, but maybe we can experiment later." Then his face turned serious. "After you tell me what's going on, Persephone."

CHAPTER THREE

O liver pushed his damp hair back, and fastened the buttons on his clean shirt. He was glad to have all that mud off.

He heard the shower in his hotel room running and glanced at the closed bathroom door. He tried *not* to think of Persephone Blake naked under the water.

And he failed spectacularly.

He'd driven back to the hotel with her in the passenger seat, still tied to him. She'd fumed silently the entire way. Ben and Cory had huddled in the back, still shocked and quiet. The rest of the team had followed in the second Jeep.

Back in his room, he'd tied Persephone to a chair while he'd showered. She'd almost stripped his skin off with the scorching glare she'd given him. After he'd showered, he'd untied her and led her into the bathroom. Once she was in the shower, he'd stolen in and taken her muddy clothes. They now sat in a soggy pile with his by the door.

He doubted even his feisty treasure hunter would attempt climbing out the bathroom window naked.

His shaken team were all resting, and Cheryl had promised to find a doctor to check Ben over.

Now it was time for Oliver to work out what the hell was going on.

The shower stopped, and he fished around in his duffel bag. He grabbed a clean khaki shirt. Then he cracked open the door an inch and held the shirt inside. A second later, it was snatched away.

Back in his room, he started pacing. He needed to know the truth. He wasn't going to risk any of the team getting hurt.

The bathroom door opened and Persephone stepped out. Her short hair was slicked back against her head and his shirt was huge on her. But not huge enough. It still left far too much of her legs gloriously bare. Oliver went hard in an instant. *Damn.* He should be thinking about gunmen and treasure hunters, not sex. Not Persephone Blake naked.

He forced his gaze from her legs to her face. He may have taken in the soft swell of her breasts on his way up. They didn't look big, but he still wanted to know what they felt like. He wanted those slim legs wrapped around his hips.

His cock pulsed. *Cool it, Ward.*

Persephone eyed the rope resting on the bed and then looked back at him. With her hair wet and thrust back off her face, she looked younger. She lifted her chin, her eyes squinting. "You going to tie me up again?"

"Not if I don't have to." He waved to the bed. "Take a seat. Time to talk."

She huffed out a breath and dropped onto the bed, crossing her arms over her chest. That just managed to pull his shirt a few inches higher on her legs.

Oliver swallowed a groan. *Focus*. He held up the plastic envelope he'd found in her muddy clothes. He tossed it on the bed, the diary page clear through the plastic. She froze.

"You're following clues listed in this diary." He shifted closer to her. "It doesn't say where it leads, but I'm guessing to some sort of treasure."

Big, gray eyes stared hard at him.

Oliver crossed his own arms. "I'm just as stubborn as you, Percy."

"Percy?"

He shrugged. "It suits you."

She sighed. "You aren't going to drop this, are you?"

"Nope."

She muttered something about stubborn archeologists. "Have you heard of the Lost Emerald Mine of the Incas?"

Oliver laughed. "A myth. The best emeralds come from Colombia, from the Muzo region. That's likely where the Inca got their emeralds."

She crossed her legs. "There have been rumors of an emerald mine in Ecuador, as well. The Spanish loved emeralds. They sent bag-loads of emeralds out on their ships with stolen Inca gold. And here in Ecuador, they sent lots of conquistadors into the jungle east of Quito, searching for *oro verde*. Green gold."

Hell. Oliver had heard the stories. "Who's diary is this?"

"It belonged to a former American soldier called Stewart Connelly. He arrived in Ecuador in 1924."

"Go on."

"He headed northeast into the jungle in search of emeralds. He was gone for months, and most considered that he'd perished." She grinned. "Then, he turned up. The missionaries at Ahuana on the Rio Napo saw a naked, emaciated, bearded, white man swimming across the river. A man wearing a bag of emeralds tied to his neck. They nursed the delirious man back to health."

Oliver uncrossed his arms. He'd heard tantalizing stories like this a hundred times before. Full of drama and few real facts.

"The man was Connelly," Percy said. "He repaid the missionaries with emeralds and headed to Quito to mount an expedition. He told everyone an amazing tale of fighting caimans and witch doctors, stumbling onto a tribe of cannibals, and of course, discovering the Lost Emerald Mine of the Inca."

"I'm sensing a *but* here."

"After stumbling around in the jungle for months, he wasn't *exactly* sure where the mine was." Her eyes were dancing as she told the story. "He had a vague list of land-marks, but that was it."

"And?"

"And, Connelly put together an expedition and headed back into the jungle."

Oliver leaned forward. "Did he find it again?"

She shook her head. "The jungle swallowed the expedition, and they were never seen again."

"Just the kind of exciting story that would excite treasure hunters." He studied her face. Her eyes were serious and her face composed. Persephone Blake was not crazy or running on adrenaline.

"I'm following the clues in the diary. They led me to your dig site. To a city on a hill and lost to the jungle."

Hell. "And the gunmen?"

She pulled her face. "I wasn't the only one to purchase the diary page. I'm harmless, but other treasure hunters..." She shrugged.

Oliver started pacing again. Persephone was not harmless, in any way, shape, or form.

This whole situation was dangerous. Suddenly, he felt angry. Angry that she was down here in the jungle alone. Angry that she would put herself in so much danger for the slimmest chance of finding treasure.

"Your family okay with you gallivanting around dangerous countries?" he bit out.

She sat back on the bed, baring more thigh. "Gallivanting?" She arched a brow. "Firstly, my family doesn't give a rat's ass about me. Secondly, I'm an adult, and I do what I want. Thirdly, I can take care of myself."

Enraged, Oliver strode closer, his legs bumping against hers. "Really? You can take care of yourself against bigger, stronger opponents?"

She looked up at him, and the next second, her legs

whipped out, knocking his own legs out from under him. Oliver went down, hitting the tile floor, hard. In the next second, Persephone was straddling his chest, shoving him back against the floor, her forearm pressed against his throat.

"Yes," she said. "Because I'm smarter."

And so damn sexy. It was probably wrong that a woman attacking him—this woman attacking him—gave him a hard-on. Damn, he was acutely aware that she was naked under his shirt. Hell, he was really hard now, his cock throbbing.

"Percy—"

She shoved her arm harder against his throat. "No one calls me nicknames."

"I do." She pushed harder and he choked.

Oliver bucked her off him. They rolled across the cool floor, smacking into the bedside table and setting it rocking.

He ended up on top, trying to keep some of his weight off her smaller body, pressing his hips against hers. She cursed, her gaze locking on his. Then, before he could figure out what she had planned, she leaned up and kissed him.

The fight went out of Oliver. She tasted so good—wild and fierce. Full of life.

She moaned, her hands moving over him and cupping his ass. He slid a hand down, cupping one of her small breasts. She was driving him crazy.

She arched into him, moaning again, and then her hands were tearing his shirt out of the waistband of his trousers.

PERSEPHONE WAS LOSING HER MIND.

Damn, Oliver Ward tasted so good, smelled so good, felt so good. The sexy fog had well and truly descended, and she was basking in it.

She smoothed her hands up his back, over lean muscles and tantalizing skin. The man had an amazing body for a scholar.

They rolled again, and for a moment, she was on top. She rubbed against him, liking the way his blue gaze flared.

"You like that?" he murmured.

"I like your body."

He rolled them again, and once again, she found herself under him. And she liked it. She didn't stop to analyze that, because she didn't ever let a man get advantage over her.

"I like yours, too." He lowered his head, his lips tracing up her neck. He nipped at her skin, and she moaned.

There was a knock at the door.

They both froze.

"Oliver?" A man's deep voice. Persephone guessed it was the older man they'd traveled with from the dig. "We're heading out to get something to eat."

Oliver muttered under his breath. "Okay, Ben. I'll catch you later."

She listened to the man's footsteps retreat. The spell between them had been broken. She shoved against

Oliver, and felt him reluctantly move off her. They both got to their feet.

"So, you're planning to find the Lost Emerald Mine of the Inca," he said. "Then what? Open a mining company in this dangerous country?"

"No." She pushed her wet hair behind her ears. "I'm planning to find the lost Incan emerald known as the Emerald Tear."

He blinked. "What?"

"Giant emerald about the size of my fist." She held up her hand and clenched it closed. "You know the legend of Tena and Fura in Colombia?"

"Yes. From the Muzo region where the emeralds come from."

"The Muzo region is named for the Muzo people. In pre-Colombian times, they mined emeralds, and told the story of Tena and Fura. They were the first man and woman made by the creator god. The god taught them how to cultivate the land, make pottery, and weave, and in order to remain immortal, they had one rule. They had to remain true to each other and not cheat."

"But Fura didn't remain faithful," Oliver said.

Percy rolled her eyes. "Just like Adam and Eve, it's all the woman's fault. A beautiful, young man called Zarbi arrived. He was looking for a specific flower, and Fura agreed to help him. Cutting to the chase, Fura and Zarbi shagged."

Oliver swallowed a laugh.

"Fura began to age, and in regret, went back to her husband. In despair, Tena stabbed himself, and Fura cried over his body. Her cries became butterflies and her tears became emeralds."

"And the creator god turned them into stone mountains that still stand in the Muzo region to this day," Oliver finished.

She leaned forward. "And here we are in a town in Ecuador called Tena. Close to where Stewart Connelly came out of the jungle in the 1920s, with a bag full of emeralds and clues leading to the lost mine. A mine where the legends say the Inca kept two giant emeralds—the Emerald Tear and the Emerald Butterfly." She shifted on her feet. "The Emerald Butterfly was allegedly stolen by the Spanish and lost."

Persephone watched Oliver thinking. A sexy little crease appeared on his brow. Damn, she could watch him think for hours. She was still tingling between her legs. This man was a *huge* distraction.

"And if you find this emerald?" he asked, his eyes serious.

She lifted her chin. "I'll sell it and retire in the Caribbean."

He watched her steadily, until his close inspection started to make her feel itchy.

"I'll help you find it," he said.

She went still. "Help me?"

"Yes."

"No. No. No." She held up her hands. "I told you, I work alone."

She was well aware of the risks she was taking. This damn job had already turned dangerous. Oliver had already had a gun pointed in his handsome face, and Persephone did *not* want to see that happen again.

"I'll work with you," he said. "Partners. All I ask is that you promise to sell the emerald to me when we find it."

She blinked, trying to find the catch. There was always a catch. He smiled. That damn smile that made her brain fog over.

"With the university and its donors' help, I'll be able to raise the funds. Besides, I think my dig is the mine workers' village."

She gasped. "What?"

"I think the town we're uncovering was where the mine workers lived. I'm guessing you need to find the next clue there."

She gave him a reluctant nod.

"So, let's work together." He held a hand out for her to shake. "We'll start first thing in the morning."

Persephone stared at his palm. He didn't have the soft hands of a man who spent all his time in the halls of academia. His hands were long-fingered and well-shaped, but he had calluses. She'd never worked with a partner. Hell, she'd never trusted anyone enough to partner with them. And she never kept a man around longer than it took for them to have a roll between the sheets.

Oliver Ward was a distraction to beat all distractions, and she already regretted what she was about to do. She took his hand.

Before she could shake, he yanked her forward so she bumped against his chest. The kiss he pressed to her lips was hard and fast. "Just wanted to seal the deal."

She shook her head. "I'm in big trouble."

He shifted, and then suddenly she felt rope on her wrist.

She looked down, staring at the rope, and she sighed. "Is that really necessary?"

He shot her that sexy smile. "I'm guessing, yes."

CHAPTER FOUR

O liver woke, blinking at the morning light filtering into his hotel room.

He rolled on the bed, the rope rubbing against the skin at his wrist.

He sat bolt upright. There was no small, sexy, infuriating treasure hunter attached to the other end of the rope.

Dammit. Scrambling off the bed, he reached for his shirt. He'd kept his trousers on to sleep, drifting off excruciatingly aware of Persephone lying beside him.

Now she was gone. The woman had managed to untie his knot and run off.

He got to the window and paused. He saw her sitting outside in the small garden, feeding bread to a gaggle of brightly colored parrots.

Slipping his feet into his shoes, he went outside. She sat on a small wooden bench, still only wearing his shirt, her hair mussed from sleep.

"I thought you'd run," he said.

She kept her gaze on the birds. "I considered it."

He sat down beside her. "Why didn't you?"

She turned her head, eyeing him. "Well, possibly I've lost my mind. Or maybe it's because I think you will actually help me find the emerald."

"So it's only about the emerald?" he asked.

She shot to her feet. "Of course."

He nodded. The little liar. He was learning to tell when she was skating close to the truth, and when she was flat-out lying.

"I think I've found your clue and the way it points."

She sucked in a breath. "Where?"

"There's a strange carving in the stonework on the hill that my student thinks is a tomb. It's had us all baffled. It shows boats and clearly points toward the Rio Napo."

Her face lit with excitement. "So, we have to follow the river." She pulled out the diary page that she'd clearly stolen back from him. "The next clue talks about a river of blood. We have to head upriver until we find a river of blood."

"River of blood. Nice," he said. "We'll need a boat."

She nodded. "Then get dressed and packed, professor."

"I'm not a professor, yet."

"But you will be, and you look like one." She winked at him. "Now, we have an Incan treasure to find." She made a shooing motion with her hands.

His gut tightened. God, she was gorgeous. It was like

there was a light shining out of her, and he wanted all that light to himself.

Inside, they both filled their backpacks. Oliver's had seen plenty of digs and expeditions, but it wasn't anywhere as battered as Persephone's. He shoved his gear, small one-man tent, and clothes in the bag, and watched Persephone duck into the bathroom to change.

Her head popped around the door. "By the way, I'm stealing this shirt. Mine's ruined."

He gave her a small salute.

When she stepped out, she had his shirt tucked into fitted, khaki pants. Oliver swallowed, desire raging inside him.

Finally, they shouldered their backpacks and headed out. "I need to tell Ben and the team that I'm leaving for a while." He knocked on the door of the neighboring room.

His mentor opened it. There was a faint bruise on his cheek from the previous day's chaos. Ben frowned at Persephone.

"I wanted to tell you that I'm heading into the jungle for a few days," Oliver said.

Ben's bushy brows drew together. "What?"

"Percy has some good leads to another Incan site that links to ours. I want to investigate it with her."

"Oliver, we had gunmen raid our site."

Oliver nodded. "And with us gone, you won't have any more trouble with them."

Ben squeezed his eyes closed. "I was afraid that was going to be the case."

"I want the team safe. Keep them working, and I'll be back as soon as I can."

Ben glanced at Persephone. "Another Incan site. And I'm guessing there's treasure involved." Ben's gaze landed back on Oliver. "This sounds like a wild-goose chase."

Oliver flashed him a smile. "It won't be. Not when I bring you back the location of the Lost Emerald Mine of the Inca."

Ben hissed out a sharp breath. "Nothing but a myth."

"I know you've been fascinated by any references to the Emerald Butterfly. It came from somewhere."

"Yes, likely from Colombia!"

"I'm going, Ben."

"Good morning," Cheryl's voice said from behind Oliver.

He turned and saw Cheryl frowning at Persephone. Then her gaze snagged on the shirt Percy was wearing, and Cheryl's lips twisted with dismay.

"What's going on?" she asked.

"Oliver is heading off on a small *side* expedition with his friend," Ben said.

Cheryl's eyes narrowed. "Really? Is that a sensible idea?"

Persephone grinned and elbowed Oliver. "Probably not. Maybe you should stay behind, professor."

He scowled down at her. "No."

Cheryl tilted her head, tossing her curls back. "You seem familiar. Do I know you?"

Persephone sketched a small bow. "Persephone Blake."

Cheryl hissed in a breath. "The infamous treasure hunter?"

Infamous? Oliver had never heard of her.

Persephone's grin widened. "I warned you."

"You discovered a cache of Aztec gold artifacts in Mexico," Cheryl said. "And sold them to the Smithsonian." There was censure in the woman's voice.

A dreamy look settled over Persephone's face. "It was a beautiful collection."

"And you found an Incan gold necklace in Peru," Cheryl added. "I suppose you sold that, too."

"It didn't match the color scheme of my wardrobe," Persephone replied simply.

Ben was staring at Persephone with an unreadable gaze. "You helped lead a team from Stanford to several unidentified temples at the Mayan city of El Mirador. It was an amazing find."

Persephone's smile slipped. "Working with them helped my own job."

"I'm friends with one of the archeologists who led the team. He said you helped them immensely."

Oliver watched Persephone shift uncomfortably. When she was trying to prove she was mercenary, she was all smiles, but when Ben paid her a compliment, she turned prickly. Interesting.

He grabbed her hand. "Percy and I will be gone for a while. I'll contact you when I get back."

"You're leaving us?" Cheryl said. "Just when we're all shaken up after the attack?"

There was a tremble in Cheryl's voice, and he caught Percy rolling her eyes.

Oliver cleared his throat. "I know. But I don't think we'll have any more trouble at the dig with Percy and me gone."

Percy nodded. "Because the bad guys will follow us, instead."

Ben shook his head and Cheryl looked shocked.

"Be careful, Oliver," Ben said.

"Always."

Oliver tugged Percy away. Out on the street, they headed toward the main footbridge across the river. Percy waved at several kids playing in the street. Down by the water's edge, lots of men stood by their boats—some fishermen, others for hire.

"Let me deal with this." With a smile, Percy strode forward and struck up a conversation with the men. It wasn't long before she had them all laughing. Oliver shook his head. There was just something about her that drew people.

Before he knew it, Percy was waving him over to a boat. The vessel wasn't big, but it wasn't small, either. Made from wood, it was long and narrow, with a spindly-looking canopy on top. A sturdy engine sat at the back.

"This is Roberto," she told him.

Oliver shook the man's hand. The man was in his mid-twenties, with a wide smile.

"Come on, Ward." Persephone climbed into the boat. "Adventure awaits. I'm going to make a treasure hunter out of you, yet."

IT WAS ALMOST PEACEFUL.

Persephone sat in the prow of the boat, watching it glide through the dark waters of the Rio Napo. She knew the river was a tributary of the mighty Amazon, and farther down, it joined with other waterways to become the majestic river.

On the water's edge, trees and vegetation grew thick. She heard birds squawk overhead and looked up as a flock of them took flight. Nearby, sitting in a tree growing out over the water, perched a red howler monkey, watching them curiously. She breathed deep, pulling in the smell of rotting leaves and the lush scent of the jungle.

She imagined Connelly passing through here, filled with excitement to find the Inca mine. Of course, the poor guy had ended up swimming across the Napo naked. She shuddered. She sure as hell wasn't planning to do that.

The quiet rustle of clothing caught her ear, and she became conscious of Oliver sitting close behind her. Okay, she'd been excruciatingly conscious of him the entire time. He'd been quiet for a while, and she liked that he seemed easy with the silence. He had a patience about him that Persephone envied. From the time she was little, she'd always felt a need to move and do and go. Her dad had always cursed her inability to sit still.

Oliver appeared to be a calming influence on her. Sitting beside him, she felt like she could just take a deep breath and enjoy the breeze on her face.

"So, any chance Roberto knows where this river of blood might be?" Oliver asked.

She shook her head, swiveling to look at him. "I asked him, but he didn't know of any rivers with red water."

More silence.

"How did you get into treasure hunting?"

Her chest tightened. "My mom."

His eyebrows rose. "She's a treasure hunter?"

"No." Persephone's hands tightened on the side of the boat. "She's a con artist and thief." Persephone glanced away, not wanting to see the shock and disgust on his face. "Once, she stole this gorgeous little amethyst brooch. It was the most beautiful thing I'd ever seen, and when I learned how old it was—crafted in England at the turn of the century—I was even more fascinated. I looked at that damn thing every day before she sold it off."

Persephone risked a glance at his face. There was a bit of shock there, but, as always, he just looked steady and considering.

"Don't worry, professor. I draw the line at being an outright criminal." Especially one who destroyed lives with a smile. Athena Blake used whatever means she could to get her job done. She didn't care who she hurt in the process.

There was a lot of her mother in her, Persephone knew that. But even she drew the line at most of the things her mother happily did for a job. Still, there was nothing you could do to escape your blood.

"Mom wasn't really around much. Dad raised me. He worked in mining, or oil and gas jobs, all around the world, but we spent a lot of time here in South America."

Oliver made a humming noise, and she wasn't sure what to make of it. She ignored her rolling stomach and forced herself to grin at him.

"I'm sure my sordid life is a whole lot different from

being a golden son raised by a wealthy father and socialite mother in Denver."

"I'm sure it is. You did your research."

"Of course."

"My parents aren't snobs." A wry smile. "Okay, maybe a little, but they aren't mean people. They were shocked, but supportive, when both of their sons went their own way. My brother is a cop and I'm an archeologist. Dad never did get the lawyer son he wanted."

"I'm sure they'll swallow their sons upholding the law and being an esteemed history professor," she said dryly. "Especially when you both eventually marry pretty socialites and give them grandkids with big, blue eyes."

Oliver laughed and Persephone couldn't look away. He had a good laugh—deep and rich. Her gaze ran down the strong column of his throat, her hands itching to touch. Something inside her tightened and warmed.

"You have it all worked out," he said.

Persephone hunched her shoulders. "It's good to know where you're headed in life."

He shifted closer. "And where are you headed, Percy?"

"I'm going to sell you the Emerald Tear and add the proceeds to my nest egg. Soon, I'm going to retire to a white-sand beach in the Caribbean. Or maybe in Polynesia. I'm not too fussy."

She pulled out her envelope and removed the picture of the beach. As Oliver reached for it, their fingers brushed. The zing of heat made her almost drop her things, and the picture of the house fell out before she could grab it. He snatched it up off the wooden bottom of the boat.

"What's this?" he asked, turning it over.

"Nothing." She tried to reach for it. "Just a house I thought looked pretty."

He eyed her. "Not sure there are many Victorian houses like this one on the beach."

She shrugged. "It's nothing. I need to throw it out. I don't even know why I kept it."

She felt his gaze on her like a physical thing. He was studying her like she was some shard of pottery he'd found in the mud and was trying to piece together.

"This looks like the restored Victorian houses in Denver."

She managed to snatch the picture out of his hand, and shoved it back into the plastic sleeve.

Roberto called out then, pointing to a sloth hanging out over the water by the river's edge, and the moment was broken.

"Oh, my God," Persephone said with a grin. "He's so cute."

The day wore on, and a couple of times, they passed other boats. The fishermen all lifted their hands in friendly waves. They spotted several small tributaries, and briefly investigated each one, but they didn't find any rivers of blood.

Soon, the sun started to set, the shadows between the trees deepening, and the sounds of the jungle changed. Persephone took her time reapplying some insect repellent, and Oliver pulled out some of the food he'd packed. She munched quietly on the trail mix, watching the jungle around them settle in for the evening. By the edge of the river, several heads popped up to watch them pass. Giant river otters.

"Oliver." She nudged him.

When he saw them, he smiled. They watched the animals until they disappeared from view.

It wasn't long before the jungle was drenched in darkness. Roberto pulled out a small flashlight and steered them over to the riverbank, where he tied the boat off on a sturdy tree branch.

"Time to get some rest," Oliver said.

Oliver pulled out his sleeping bag, and Persephone did the same. At the end of the boat, Roberto pulled out a blanket and curled up on the wooden bottom, looking like he'd done it a hundred times before.

The boat wasn't large, so there wasn't a lot of room. Oliver was already lying down, and Persephone had no choice but to lie beside him.

The sleeping bag didn't give much protection from the wooden floor, and she wiggled around to get comfortable. She'd slept in far worse places. She shifted again, her body brushing against Oliver. She went still.

A strong arm wrapped around her and yanked her back. His chest was pressed to her back, and he pressed his legs against hers. "Quit moving."

"Trying to get comfortable."

"This is comfortable." He rested his face against her hair. "Go to sleep."

There was no way she could sleep all tangled up with sexy Oliver Ward. She felt his hand move and then he was playing with her hair. It felt...nice.

47

Before she knew it, Persephone dozed off.

When she woke, she was drenched in sunlight and her face was pressed into a hard wall of male chest.

She blinked. *Oh, God*. They were wrapped up in each other, his arm draped over her waist, her leg nestled between his. Damn, they fit together perfectly.

"Good morning." His voice was a deep rumble.

Desire shot through her. He was so damn gorgeous, and with him right there in her face, how the hell was she supposed to resist him?

He fiddled with her hair again and she dragged in a deep breath. Touching him just a little bit wouldn't hurt, right? "Morning."

Then she heard whistling. She turned her head and spotted their guide cheerfully tinkering with the boat's motor.

Reluctantly, she pulled herself away from Oliver's body and sat up. Sunlight glinted brilliantly off the water, and the air was thick with humidity today.

As Oliver pulled his boots on and rolled away from the sleeping bags, Persephone washed her face and ran her fingers through her hair. She snorted. She bet Cheryl was spending more time doing her hair.

After a quick, simple breakfast, Roberto started the engine and pulled them out onto the river.

"We might find it today," Oliver said.

She nodded. If the damn river of blood was around here, they'd damn well find it.

No more than an hour had passed, when they rounded a wide curve in the river. Suddenly, a larger boat appeared, black smoke chugging out of its stack. There was a large machine gun mounted on the front.

"*Bandidos.*" Roberto waved at Oliver and Persephone to sit down lower.

"Shit." Oliver grabbed her and they sank lower, trying not to draw any attention to themselves.

But the gunboat turned, aiming directly at them. Roberto leaned out, shouting and waving his arms.

The gunboat didn't slow down. Persephone saw men in fatigues on the deck, one of them moving in behind the machine gun.

"Oliver!"

"I see." His fingers tightened on her hand.

The gunboat opened fire.

The roar of the machine gun drowned out everything else. Persephone couldn't even scream. In horror, she watched bullets tear into Roberto's body.

Suddenly, Oliver grabbed Persephone and yanked her backward over the side of their boat. They fell into the river with a splash.

CHAPTER FIVE

O liver kicked hard, cursing as he gulped in and spat out river water. He kept a tight hold on Percy as her head popped up and she dragged in air.

Behind them, the roar of machine-gun fire was deafening, as bullets tore into their boat.

"Swim." He shoved Persephone toward the shore. "Head for the bank."

The boat gave them some protection, but they needed to get out of there. *Fast*. He tried not to think of the caimans in the river.

Together, he and Percy stayed low in the water and swam hard.

Bullets whizzed into the water nearby, and Percy yelped. He shoved her ahead of him, and a second later, they reached the bank. Thankfully, it was flatter here than by the dig, and they easily scrambled out of the water. More bullets slammed into the mud at their feet, and this time, Percy cried out.

Oliver gave her another push and they charged into the foliage.

Thank God he'd had the presence of mind to grab his backpack before he'd pulled Percy into the water. He pulled his machete off it and then slung the sodden pack onto his back.

Behind them, shouts echoed near the river bank. The bastards were following them.

"Keep moving," he said. "We need to put as much distance between them and us as we can."

She nodded, pushing her sopping hair back off her forehead. Her shirt was plastered to her chest, outlining her breasts.

God, Ward, not the time.

"Are you going to cut a path for us?" she asked.

He shook his head. "We'll go as far as we can without doing that. I don't want to leave them an easy trail to follow."

She straightened her shoulders and set off, pushing vines out of her way. Oliver followed, smiling. She was a trooper, his Percy. No crying, no complaining, she just got on with it.

They went for an hour, both of them sweating heavily. The vegetation had thickened, and the air was heavy and still, with no breeze to ease the pressure. He stopped and made her take a drink. When they were moving again, he started using the machete.

It took a few swings, but he finally found a rhythm, hacking at the vines and branches. Where they could ease through, he didn't slash, trying to obscure their trail.

As they continued onward, they paused frequently to

listen. There were no sounds of pursuit. He hoped to hell the bastards in the gunboat had given up.

"Poor Roberto." There was grief on Percy's face.

Her chin was on her chest, and Oliver took a second to wrap an arm around her and give her a quick hug. "When we get back to Tena, we'll alert the authorities and contact his family."

She nodded. They trekked on, but Oliver knew the adrenaline that had initially fueled them was draining away. Still, they needed to keep moving for now.

Suddenly, thunder cracked overhead and the rain started. It wasn't long before they were both soaked. Percy looked miserable, although she didn't utter a single complaint.

He tried to estimate how much distance they'd put between them and their attackers. Was it enough? He sure as hell didn't want to risk her life.

"I have never been this wet and muddy before," Percy said with a scowl.

They hadn't gone much farther when the muted roar he thought was the rain got louder. He tilted his head and listened. No, not the rain. He knew what it was.

He grabbed Persephone's hand and yanked her onward. They broke out of the foliage, and up ahead, he saw a gorgeous waterfall tumbling down over dark rocks.

"Holy shit," she breathed.

He smiled at her reaction, but when he looked at her, he realized she wasn't entranced by the waterfall. In fact, she was staring in the opposite direction.

Oliver turned. The rain had stopped now, the sun

valiantly trying to break out from behind the thick clouds. Every muscle in his body locked.

They were looking down at a narrow valley, and the beautiful sweep of a river. A *red* river.

"The rocks down there must have iron or something in them," Percy said. "It turns the water red."

Oliver stared at the dark crimson ribbon. "Hell."

She turned, grinning widely at him. "We found it! The river of blood."

She leaped on him, her legs wrapping around his hips, and her lips smacking against his.

Oliver wrapped his arms around her, tilting his head and deepening the kiss. She tasted so good and he wanted more. She smelled like rain and tasted like honey.

They broke apart, but he kept an arm wrapped around her. "What's the next clue after the river of blood?"

"It said to follow the river to some black cliffs." Her lips turned into a frown.

"Hmm."

She peered at him, her brow creased. "What?"

He gripped her shoulders and turned her toward the waterfall. "You mean, like those cliffs?"

She sucked in a breath, taking in the dark rocks. They both looked up, staring at the long, graceful fall of water that was sliding over black cliffs.

"Oh, my God." Her smile was incandescent, excitement shining off her. "We're so close!"

"Maybe, but right now, we need to clean off, eat, and get some fresh clothes on."

She looked like she wanted to argue, but finally

nodded. Together, they made their way over to the waterfall. The falls landed on smooth, flat rocks, which slanted downward, creating a shallow pool.

Oliver dropped his pack. That water looked damned good.

"You wash up first." Percy pulled some things from his backpack. "You've been the one swinging the machete for hours."

"You saying I smell?"

She grinned. "I didn't say that, professor."

With a nod, he waded into the water and headed for the waterfall. He watched the mud slide off his clothes. He'd need to rinse them off and see if he could get them dry. He had a spare set in his bag, and he could loan Percy a shirt, but not trousers.

Stepping under the edge of the spray, he tilted his face up and stripped off his shirt. His trousers and underwear followed, and he tossed them on a rock. Naked, he stepped under the spray. Damn, what a day. They'd been shot at, and an innocent man had died. He and Percy had almost been killed. And it was likely the bad guys were still after them.

He let the spray beat down over his body. Even with everything they'd faced over the last few hours, Oliver had never felt so alive.

He opened his eyes, and his gaze landed on Persephone, perched on a rock by the water's edge. Gray eyes were locked on him. She was watching him—completely unashamed and unabashed.

His cock hardened. Every cell in his body roared to life. Okay, *now* he felt alive.

He finished washing out his hair, and he watched the way her gaze followed his movements. There was hunger on her pretty face.

This wild, vibrant woman wanted him.

Desire beat hotly in Oliver's blood. He slid his palm over his stomach and took his cock in hand. He stroked himself.

Percy's lips parted, her hungry gaze on his hand.

Unable to stop, Oliver kept pumping his cock. He imagined it was her touching him. Her gaze never wavered from his hand and cock. She didn't look away shyly or pretend she hadn't seen.

No, Persephone Blake was direct, and she always went after what she wanted.

He watched as she slid off the rock and jumped into the water, fully clothed. She started swimming toward him.

PERSEPHONE HAD LEARNED PRETTY EARLY in life to not want too many things. To not care too much.

People had left her disappointed too many times, and she'd learned the hard way that things you cared about could easily be lost or snatched away. Too often, she'd been left empty-handed.

Nope, life had taught her to depend on herself. If you did want something, you went after it yourself, and you tried not to care about it too much.

Right now, all she wanted was Oliver Ward.

She wanted every glorious, firm inch of him. And dammit, she cared. Too much.

Pushing through the water, she let her gaze run over his muscled body. He wasn't musclebound, like he was always in the gym, but he clearly worked out and took care of himself. He had the body of an athlete, with a firm chest, muscular arms, and toned abs. He was seriously screwing up her stereotype of a stuffy historian.

She swallowed, need pumping through her, leaving her lightheaded and breathless. Screw it all. She was done being careful. Right now, she was throwing caution to the wind.

She reached him and stepped up onto the flat rock he was standing on.

God, he looked even better up close. She didn't know if he grabbed her or if she grabbed him, but suddenly they were kissing. She pressed her palms to his slick chest, and his hands were tearing at her clothes.

He made short work of her shirt and bra, tossing them onto a nearby rock. Then strong arms wrapped around her, lifting her up. She slid her hands into his wet hair just as he lifted her a few inches higher. He licked one of her nipples and sucked it into his mouth.

"Yes." Her hands twisted in his hair.

"I've wanted to do that ever since I first laid eyes on you." He sucked on her nipple, tongue lapping.

Sensation exploded through Persephone and she moaned.

"I've been half hard ever since you crashed into my life," he growled.

She was panting now. "Only half?"

He growled again. "Not right now."

He set her down and opened her trousers. A second later, he skimmed them down her legs. *Yes.* She needed to be naked. She needed to feel this man against her, skin to skin.

She kicked the trousers away, and Oliver grabbed them before the water washed them into the depths of the pool. He tossed them with the rest of their clothes.

Naked, they stood there, staring at each other. Water washed over his skin in rivulets. She watched the streams run down, past his rock-hard cock that was standing firm against his belly. Down the strong columns of his thighs.

She reached for his cock. His beautiful, smooth cock. She started stroking it.

"Not so fast," he ground out.

"Now. I need you." She felt so damn needy. She needed him to douse this fire.

"I don't want to rush it," Oliver said, his mouth nipping her neck.

For Persephone, sex had always been quick, fun tumbles. She looked into his blue eyes and saw some emotion churning there. This...this was something else.

He scooped her up and then walked through the curtain of water. A ledge of flat rock sat behind it. He set her on it, the falling curtain of water giving them a sense of privacy.

She looked into his eyes. They were so intense. So possessive.

Something inside her stuttered and she reached for his cock. "I need you inside me."

She knew they only had this moment. This adventure. A man like Oliver Ward would never stay around. Not with a woman like her. She felt a sharp pain somewhere around the region of her heart.

Then he was kissing her again. His warm lips caressed her breasts, and he sucked on her nipples until she was panting. This wasn't what she was used to. Emotions battered at her and she tried to reach for him again. His talented mouth moved down her belly, and she arched up. Then, he was nudging her legs apart.

"We aren't fucking fast and hard, Percy." Before she could draw a breath, his mouth was on her, licking at her folds.

Oh. God. He started sucking, his mouth finding her swollen clit.

"I'm going to worship you. Going to drive you wild."

Panic fluttered in her chest. She liked control. "I...can't."

"Yes, you can." He groaned against her and kept licking.

Persephone didn't have time to prepare herself. Her orgasm was roaring closer, with every lick and suck. It was like being tossed into the air with no safety net. She ground herself against his mouth, crying out his name. The pleasure was too much.

Persephone exploded.

When she was able to see again, she was sprawled on the rock, Oliver's tense face above hers.

Desire was etched deep on his face, his lips still glistening with her juices. She'd never seen anything so sexy. She reached for him.

His big body moved, nudging between her legs. She

lifted her head and watched as he notched his cock between her thighs.

"I don't have any condoms." His voice was a gritty rasp.

Persephone knew her body well, and if she'd learned anything about Oliver, it was that he was a good, trustworthy man.

"Come inside me, Oliver. I need you."

He lunged forward, his cock lodging deep.

Her mouth opened. "Oliver!"

"Take me." He shoved into her again.

Persephone felt her body stretching to accommodate him. "I am."

He pressed his hands to the rock on either side of her, taking her with wild thrusts. Her charming scholar was gone, and in his place was a hard, ruthless lover with need riding him. Need for *her*.

This wasn't sex or loving. This was a possession.

Persephone wrapped her legs around his hips. As this big, gorgeous man moved inside her, something deep within her trembled.

Then the heated sensations started to build inside her again. She gripped him tighter, husky cries ripping from her throat and echoing in the air. She reached up, wrapping her arms around him. As another orgasm exploded through her, she opened her mouth to scream. But his lips were there, swallowing her cry. She raked his back with her nails.

With another hard thrust and a deep groan, he came inside her.

CHAPTER SIX

W*hat the hell was that?* Oliver's chest was working like bellows. *Jesus.*

He tried to get his legs functioning again. He managed to lever himself off Persephone's prone body. Her eyes were closed, her head turned to the side, and her face flushed.

He lifted her and lowered them both down into the water. When his cock slipped out of her, she moaned.

Dammit, he was still hard. That had never happened before, even when he'd been a randy teenager.

Suddenly, Oliver felt a violent need to imprint his claim on this woman. To show her that she belonged to *him.* He was well aware that Persephone Blake lived her life on her own terms and depended on no one. Hell, it was one of the things he admired about her.

But he wanted her to trust him. To depend on *him.*

The primal need beat through him. The thought of

her waltzing away from him after this, like what they shared meant nothing, made him growl.

"Oliver?"

He gripped her hips, turned her around, and pressed her belly against the rock where he'd just fucked her. Her pretty ass was out of the water, and he stroked the firm curves of it. She made a low sound, pushing back against his palms. He slid his hand down, stroking between her thighs. He found her clit, rolling it between his fingers.

She jerked and let out a deep, husky cry. She looked back at him over her shoulder. "You still raring to go?" She licked her lips. "Professor, you are full of surprises."

Her tone was teasing, but there was something serious in her eyes. He pushed two fingers inside her and her body clenched on him.

"Brace yourself." His voice was guttural.

She froze, her breath coming in pants. "You look...dangerous."

"I'd never hurt you, Percy. But right now, I'm going to fuck you hard."

She licked her lips again and opened her legs, pushing her ass back at him.

Oliver growled, gripping her hips. He watched as she pressed her cheek to the stone. In surrender to him.

He leaned forward and slammed his cock inside her.

She grunted and pushed back. "More."

He started pumping into her. She was wet and tight and glorious. Merciless desire drove him, like the primal beat of the jungle had ignited something deep inside.

But he knew it was all Percy.

As he thrust inside her, Oliver lost track of time. He

lost track of how many times she'd climaxed.

Sensations gathered inside him—hot, hard, unstoppable. With a shout, his release rolled through him and he came again with a deep roar.

"God." He collapsed on her. Unable to do more, he tangled his hand in her hair and turned her face toward him. He pressed a soft kiss to her lips.

"Not quite the mild-mannered archeologist I thought you were," she murmured sleepily.

He pressed his lips to hers again. "Not with you, sweetheart."

Right then, Percy's stomach growled. Oliver pressed a kiss to her bare shoulder and felt another feeling overtake him. The need to take care of her.

"I'd better feed you." He tried to pretend that the Earth hadn't just shifted under his feet, and stood. "Then, we'd better keep moving. I'd be happier if we put some more distance between us and our *friends* before we find someplace to camp for the night."

She stood, heedless of the fact that she was naked. She scooped up some water and splashed it against her chest.

His gaze slipped down, taking in her small, firm breasts and noticing a few red patches where the rock had abraded her skin. He gently pulled her into the water and took over splashing water on her. As he gently washed between her legs, she watched him, her cheeks pink.

Persephone had no problem with raunchy sex, but anything approaching intimacy appeared to scare her.

She'd been alone a long time. He was planning to

change that.

Back on the riverbank, they set their clothes out to dry. Oliver pulled on fresh clothes and offered her a clean shirt. They ate together, sitting on the edge of the pool, both of them staring down at the red river below.

"So, what's our next move?" He arched his head to look at the black cliffs towering above them.

She pointed upward. "We need to get up there."

He frowned. "Have you got some secret climbing gear that I don't know about?"

"Nope." She grinned. "But we don't need it. Look." She pointed behind him.

Oliver swiveled. He looked at the black rocks of the cliff. They were overgrown with vines and other plants. "What?"

Percy bounded up and gently pushed some vines back.

He hissed in a breath. "Damn."

Crude stairs had been cut into the cliff face. They were old and weathered by time. The vines, moss, and other growth had almost completely obscured them. But not, it seemed, from Percy's eagle eyes.

"Fancy a bit of hot, sweaty exertion?" she asked.

"I think we already exerted ourselves in the waterfall."

She smiled. "True."

He stood and grabbed his backpack and machete. "But yes, I'm ready."

They quickly packed up. Oliver watched Percy pull her damp trousers back on and wince, but she didn't complain.

At the base of the stairs, Oliver hacked away at the vines.

"Let's go," he said.

The stairs were rough and wet. In places, old, rotting leaves had accumulated. It was a slick and dangerous climb.

Halfway up, Oliver was soaked in sweat, and his muscles were burning. But then he heard Percy laugh.

He looked back at her. She was having the time of her life, and he smiled. With this woman by his side, Oliver had never felt so alive.

PERSEPHONE WOKE UP, once again plastered against Oliver's bare chest.

He was still asleep, and she took the chance to look at him without the full force of his blue eyes and personality shining on her.

The man was so handsome. He had strong bones that would help him age well.

She shifted a little, feeling an avalanche of aches and twinges come alive in her body. Some from their mad jungle dash and the harrowing, slow climb up the cliff. Some from Oliver sliding that sizable cock of his inside her body.

Persephone released a long breath. By the time they'd made it to the top of the cliff, daylight was already waning, and they'd both been tired. They'd decided to set up the small tent and get some rest.

The tent was only designed for one, so it was a tight

fit, but Oliver made the most of it. He ended up getting her naked again and had her screaming against his mouth. She blew out a shuddering breath. It hadn't been sex or fucking, which were the only things Persephone had experience with. What she and Oliver had done had been something else. Something that scared her.

She shook her head, lifting a hand to stroke his cheek, his stubble scratchy under her fingers. It didn't scare her enough to back away. She couldn't keep him, but she could enjoy him while he was hers. After this crazy adventure, Dr. Oliver Ward would go back to Denver, be the darling of his university, marry a well-bred woman, and have a nice, sensible life.

Persephone swallowed against the rock in her throat. He was so beautiful, his handsome face relaxed in sleep.

A fierce, hot feeling burned in her chest. For now, he was hers, and she was taking everything she could get. Making memories that she could take out and cherish when she was sitting on her white-sand beach.

She stroked her hands down his chest, sliding down his body. She pressed a kiss to his hipbone before she cupped his beautiful cock. She wasted no time sucking him into her mouth.

He woke with a groan.

"Percy." His hand clenched in her hair, but he didn't pull her off him, or take over. He let her keep working him, licking and sucking.

She felt how tense he was, his body on the edge, and about to come. Then he yanked her upward, pulling her to straddle him.

He was flat on his back, and Persephone lifted her hips and sank down on his cock.

They both groaned, and then Oliver curled up, rising to kiss her. She moved her hips, riding him slowly, and their gazes locked. His eyes didn't move away from hers as they made love. She took him deep inside her body, savoring the growing warmth in her belly.

She heard his breathing change, and the sensations in her coalesced to a sharp point.

"Percy." His hands clamped on her hips, driving her down.

Her climax raced through her, and they both cried out. As she came, she felt him spurting inside her.

When she could think again, her head was resting on his broad shoulder.

Oliver pressed a kiss to her temple. "Much as I'd like to stay like this all day, we have an emerald to find."

Percy moved off him, her body clenching and feeling strangely empty. She pulled out her envelope and showed him the diary page. "The next clue says to head toward three snow-covered mountains."

He nodded. They'd spotted the three mountains in the distance, from the top of the cliff before the sun had set. He curved a hand over her hip. "Then I suggest unless you want mosquito bites all over that creamy skin, you get dressed."

They worked well together, grabbing some quick breakfast and packing up the tent. Oliver wouldn't let her carry the backpack, but Persephone insisted taking a turn with the machete.

They moved steadily through the dense jungle.

When her muscles started to ache, Oliver took over. Damn, she could watch the flex of his muscles under his shirt all day long.

They took turns a few more times. The cool, refreshing waterfall was now a distant memory, and Persephone felt tired, hot, and sweaty.

"Drink break," Oliver said.

She lowered the machete to the muddy ground. He moved over to a fallen log and opened the backpack. He pulled out the water, tipping it back to take a drink.

A flash of movement caught Persephone's eye. She moved fast, adrenaline surging through her bloodstream. She rammed into Oliver, knocking him aside.

The snake struck out, missing its target. Persephone swung the machete, bringing it down to behead the reptile.

"Fuck." Oliver stared at the dead snake. "Looks like some sort of pit viper."

Persephone's heart was still racing. She took in the snake's brown-and-black markings. "Either a lancehead or a bushmaster."

"Both of which are highly venomous." He looked at her. "If it had bitten me, I would have been dead."

Her gut rolled. "I like you alive."

He leaned down and pressed a hard kiss against her lips. "I like being alive."

They kept going, but as Persephone hacked away at the vines and foliage, all she kept seeing in her head was Oliver dying from a snake bite. Dammit, she hated even the idea of it.

Suddenly, the machete hit rock, and pain reverberated up her arm.

Oliver pushed up beside her, shoving some vines aside.

They both froze, Persephone's heart pounding in her ears. It was a carved stone statue.

A lot of the statue had been worn away by rain, and time, and the jungle, but it was clearly a standing man, wearing some sort of headdress, his hands clasped in front of him.

"Definitely Incan." Oliver's face was alive with excitement.

Carefully, she cut more vines away. Not too far away, stood another similar statue.

"Down here." He kicked at the mud and dead leaves on the ground. She helped him clear the space, and saw the stones embedded into the muddy ground. It was a path.

Together, they followed it, hacking away more vegetation.

More statues lined the pathway, all standing men with different headdresses. Finally, the path ended at a cliff face.

"Oliver, look."

There was a collapsed entrance leading into the rock, with Incan carvings around it. It had to be the entrance to the mine.

Oliver grabbed her hand, grinning. "We did it! We found the Lost Emerald Mine of the Inca."

She smiled back at him. "Well, it's not lost anymore."

CHAPTER SEVEN

O liver felt a surge of exhilaration. His job was usually made up of small wins and discoveries. But this...this was huge.

He absolutely understood what had attracted Percy to being a treasure hunter. The never-ending thrill of the chase, and then discovering something like this—something that had been lost to time for so long.

He studied the classic Incan carvings, trying to memorize all the details. There was a part of him that liked these just as much. The record of a people who'd once thrived here, with a rich, vibrant history. For him, the small things, even ones that weren't so shiny, were exciting, too.

"Looks like the mine caved in a long time ago," Oliver said. "The Emerald Tear could be buried."

Percy frowned, but shook her head. "The diary says that the Tear and Butterfly were kept on statues outside the mine. That's how the Butterfly went missing and ended up in the hands of the Spanish."

Oliver moved some vines, keeping a wary eye out for snakes. He discovered more statues, and together they checked each one. There was no sign of precious jewels.

Then he spied a crumbling stone archway that led away from the mine entrance. "Look."

With the machete, he hacked away at the plants, and they saw another stone path, partly buried in the mud.

Percy stepped up beside him. "Let's check it out."

Together, they followed the trail. The path soon veered uphill, heading up above the mine.

"There's another statue," she said. "Wow. Oliver, check this out!"

He watched as she cleared the vines away from the carved stone. He sucked in a breath. The statue's chest was dotted with small, uncut emeralds. "Incredible." Each precious gem was the size of his thumbnail.

Percy circled the statue and pulled a face. "No Emerald Tear."

He didn't think she sounded too upset. Something told him that she was just as excited as he was as finding the mine.

A sudden burst of gunfire shattered the quiet. Oliver dove at Percy, and saw bullets hitting the dirt nearby. They both crashed to the ground.

Shit. They were stuck on this narrow path, halfway up a hillside. He turned, and watched as armed bandits appeared, all wearing fatigues and cradling weapons.

A man wearing a khaki shirt tucked into dark-green trousers, and shiny, brown boots appeared. He was fit and lean, and looked to be about forty years old. His blond hair gleamed, and he smiled at them like they were old friends. He waved at the gunmen.

Oliver and Percy were jerked to their knees, and a man ripped the machete out of Oliver's hands. A second later, he felt the cold barrel of a gun pressed against the back of his neck. Out of the corner of his eye, he could see one digging into Percy's, as well. His gut tightened. *Dammit to hell.*

"I was having some trouble deciphering the clues," the man said, in a crisp, British accent. "But you two made it a lot easier for me. We practically followed you all the way here."

"Who the hell are you?" Percy snapped.

The stranger tipped his bush hat at them. "Forgive me. Where are my manners? I'm Henry Acton. I'm the man who's going to make a fortune selling the Emerald Tear."

"Treasure hunter," Oliver spat. "No respect for history."

The man raised his blond brows. "And yet you're fucking one, Dr. Ward." His dark gaze moved to Percy. "She might be prettier than me, but do you really think you can trust her?"

"The Emerald Tear isn't here," Oliver said.

The man's pleasant smile slipped into something ugly. The man pulled a large knife off his belt. "I beg to differ, Dr. Ward."

Acton moved closer to Percy and Oliver felt his heart start pounding. She lifted her chin defiantly.

"Little Persephone knows where it is, don't you, darling?" the man drawled.

Oliver looked at her. Her face was blank and she was watching the man steadily.

What the hell was the asshole talking about?

"See, Persephone here is like me," Acton said silkily. "She doesn't show all her cards, and she trusts no one. Even the man sharing her bed."

Oliver's stomach hardened. "No." He was sure she'd been starting to trust him.

He saw Percy flinch and her head turned his way. Her eyes were pleading. "Oliver—"

"Tell us the final clue, Ms. Blake. The one you didn't share with Mr. Ward. The one that the old, cunning dealer Sosa gave you and refused to tell me."

"No," she said.

Acton lifted the knife, bringing it close to her throat. "Even when I tortured Sosa quite creatively, he wouldn't tell me. I wonder how long you'll last."

Shit. Oliver watched Percy's face go pale.

"I have nothing to tell you, asshole," she snapped.

Acton pressed the knife against her cheek. "Really?"

She glared at him. "It doesn't matter what you do to me, I won't tell you anything."

"Oh, I'm not going to do anything to you." The man spun and suddenly stabbed the knife into Oliver's shoulder.

Burning pain spiked through him, and Oliver grunted. *Fucking bastard.* He stared at the blade piercing his skin.

Percy cried out. Acton yanked the knife out and stabbed Oliver's shoulder again.

Oliver gritted his teeth against the pain. Blood bloomed on his shirt.

"Talk," Acton said. "Or I'll make you watch him bleed to death right here in the mud."

PANIC POURED through Persephone like acid in her veins.

She stared at the bright, red blood soaking into Oliver's shirt. Good, smart, handsome Oliver Ward. He was far too good for her.

Acton lifted the knife again. Persephone tasted bile in her throat, and felt like she was going to vomit. "Stop!"

Acton lowered the knife and smiled at her. Oliver was refusing to look at her. His gaze was on the ground, one hand pressed to his wounds.

"I'll tell you," she said. "Stop hurting him and I'll tell you."

"So disappointing, Ms. Blake. I was sure you were the perfect, cold-hearted bitch."

She glared at the man.

Acton tilted his head back and laughed. "God, I think it's worse than I thought. You're in love with him."

She jerked. Out of the corner of her eye, she saw Oliver's head snap up, but she couldn't look at him. She felt exposed.

"Tell me the final clue," Acton demanded.

Dragging in a shuddering breath, she told him, "The emeralds rest with a bird's-eye view of the mine."

The man nodded. "So, they're up on the cliffs somewhere." He jerked his head at one of the guards and suddenly a man yanked Persephone to her feet and shoved her forward. Another guard grabbed the back of Oliver's shirt and dragged him up.

They moved in single file up the path. It got steeper and rockier, as well as muddier and more slippery. More weathered statues dotted the vegetation. She kept glancing at Oliver. He wouldn't meet her gaze, but she could see he was in pain. Blood stained his shirt and the hand he was holding over the wounds.

I'm so sorry, Oliver.

They paused on a flat ledge, and Persephone turned her head. From here, they had a beautiful view over the river below. The mine entrance was hidden somewhere in the jungle beneath them.

She was shoved forward again, and ahead, two guards slashed at the vegetation with machetes. Not long after, the jungle gave way to a wide, stone platform.

She sucked in an awed breath. It was clearly manmade, and in the center, perched two huge stone statues.

Both statues wore elaborate half-circle headdresses. One had large, circular earrings that she could see were made of a mass of small emeralds and gold. In the center of the headdress was a large, irregular-shaped, empty space.

Where a butterfly-shaped emerald had probably once sat.

On the other statue, right in the center of the head-dress, was a huge, tear-shaped emerald.

Murmurs broke out. Instantly, Persephone imagined the Incas standing here, honoring their traditions and beliefs. A sense of history descended on her, and she understood what drove Oliver's passion for his discipline.

She looked up. Above the platform, the Inca had done some simple masonry and earthwork to keep rocks and mud from sliding into their sacred place. But over the years, layers of dirt and mud had built up, and it now all perched perilously on the cliff ledge above.

She looked at Oliver and saw that he wasn't looking at the statues. He was looking at her, his face unreadable.

Yes, Acton was right. She was falling in love with Oliver Ward. It was foolish, but she didn't know how to stop herself.

What she did know, however, was that she wasn't letting Acton take the Emerald Tear, no matter what. And she sure as hell wasn't letting the bastard hurt Oliver again.

She glanced up and watched as Acton climbed up the base of the sculpture. Using his knife, he pried the Emerald Tear out of the statue. He stood there grinning, holding the magnificent stone in his hand.

It should be in a museum. More than just this asshole deserved to see it.

She glanced around. There were four armed men. The odds sucked, but she'd always enjoyed a risk or two.

Still, she didn't want to risk Oliver's life. *Think, Perse-phone, think.*

"Acton?" she called out. "What about the very final clue?"

The man frowned. "What?"

"Sosa didn't tell you there was another emerald?" She hoped her tone sounded seductive.

"No."

Shrugging off her guard, she sauntered close to Acton. "I'll tell you, but you have to let me in on the deal."

She felt Oliver watching her, his gaze boring right between her shoulder blades. She was certain that he hated her right now. But she was getting him out of here alive, whatever it took.

She glanced at him, trying to pour everything she was thinking and feeling into her gaze. Then she focused back on Acton, seemingly paying no attention to the nearby guards.

"I'm listening, but you must talk fast." The man's gaze narrowed at her. "I'm just about done with the two of you."

"There's an emerald even bigger than this one, not far from here..."

Persephone took one more step forward, then, in a lightning-quick move, she reached over and grabbed the guard's pistol from his holster. She lifted it and fired at the guard. He fell backward into the vegetation.

Swiveling, she crouched and fired at the next guard, and the one beside him.

She heard Acton shouting and turned back. Acton was charging down from the statue.

"Kill her!" he screamed.

But the fourth guard had headed back down the path, searching for cover, and tugging Oliver with him.

"Percy!" Oliver yelled. He struggled against the guard, and she saw the man's gun go flying into the bushes.

Acton slipped and fell onto his knees, but he jumped back up, his gaze zeroed in on the path down the hillside.

He was going to get away with the emerald. *Hell, no.* Percy looked up where the rocks and mud sat above the platform—years of accumulation. She took aim and fired.

She kept firing. Nothing happened.

Dammit, come on. Forcing her hands to stay steady, she pulled the trigger again.

Several small rocks tumbled down the side of the hill, and pinged off the stone platform. More followed, and the ground vibrated beneath them.

"You'll kill us all," Acton yelled, slipping as he tried to get back to the path.

One injured guard was up on his knees, holding his wounded chest and staring in horror. A large boulder broke free and started to roll down the hill, straight toward them, rapidly gathering speed.

Oh, shit. Persephone dodged. The giant rock rushed by her, slammed into the guard, and took him over the edge of the cliff. He screamed as he fell.

Acton was running, clutching the emerald. Persephone chased after him. Smaller rocks were rolling across the ground, making her progress difficult. She leaped over them, trying to stay on her feet.

Then the ground started to rumble. A deep-throated roar grew around them.

She glanced up and her eyes widened. Holy hell, the entire side of the mountain was coming loose. *Mudslide.*

The mass slowly shifted, oozing downward and gathering speed. Coming right at her.

"Percy!"

Oliver's shout made her turn. He was standing pressed against the side of the cliff, in a small alcove, near the carved steps. He was out of the path of the mudslide. He held a hand outstretched to her.

She raced toward him, slipping on the small rocks littering the space. The final guard was still standing there, frozen in shock. There was no sign of Acton.

The mud rushed closer. She looked back and saw the slide was almost on her. It swallowed the guard and swept him away.

She wasn't going to make it.

Despair filled her. She was going to die here.

Her gaze locked on Oliver's and then her eyes widened. "No."

He was charging toward her.

"No!" she yelled at him.

His strong arms wrapped around her, and he picked her up like she was a football. He sprinted back toward the alcove. The mud was rushing at them, no more than a meter away.

Oliver tightened his grip on her and jumped.

They slammed into the rock face, safe, both of them grunting and scrabbling for purchase on the rocky surface. The mud rushed past, pouring over the cliff and down the hill.

CHAPTER EIGHT

"Thanks."

Percy's voice was shaky. Oliver kept them pressed against the rock. The mudslide was slowing now, but he wasn't taking any chances.

He looked down. Percy was staring at her muddy boots.

"Did you think I was going to let you fucking die?" Anger flooded him.

Her head snapped up. "You could have been killed! You shouldn't have rushed into the path of a mudslide."

He gripped her shoulders, ignoring the sharp sting of his stab wounds. "Stay safe and let you get killed?"

She lifted one shoulder. "Your life is worth way more than mine."

His anger flared. "I never want to hear you say that again. If you think I couldn't see that you were lying to that asshole to get us out of there, then you aren't as clever as I thought you were."

Percy swallowed. "I didn't tell you everything, though. I'm not a good person, Oliver. I'm not like you."

"I'm not some damn saint, Percy. And you're not the devil." He shook his head. "We all have shades of gray. We can always do better and make better choices." He reached out and pulled her close. He needed her close.

She pressed her face to his shirt, and he slid a hand into her hair. She was alive. That was all that mattered.

"You should forget about me," she whispered. "Find some well-read, educated woman who suits you."

"Who'll cook me a nice meal every night and bring me my slippers? Is that what you think I want?"

She shrugged her shoulder again.

"I beg to differ. I like getting muddy, and hacking through the jungle, and making love under a waterfall."

She looked up at him and her chest hitched.

"I'm falling for you, Persephone Blake."

Shock crossed her face. "What? No. I..." She pressed her lips together, opened her mouth, then closed it again.

Oliver kind of enjoyed watching her stumble over herself. "Persephone Blake, speechless?"

It was amusing, but he also felt a hollow sensation carving him out inside. Percy felt like the wind. Something wild and free, and impossible to hold in his hands.

"We need to stop Acton getting away with the emerald." She straightened. "We don't have time for this right now."

Oliver sighed. "Agreed." His hands tightened on her. "But we *will* talk about this."

He grabbed her hand and pulled her down the path. They climbed down the mud-drenched trail as quickly as they dared. He wondered how far ahead Acton was. Had he been caught by the slide? Did the bastard have transport close by?

Suddenly, a dark shape leaped out from a tree and slammed into Oliver. They skidded through the dirt, and pain roared through Oliver's injuries. Nausea rose, and he struggled to push it back and fight.

He rolled over...just in time to see Acton aiming a punch at him. *Fuck*. Oliver jerked his body, and they rolled again.

They wrestled in the undergrowth, the mud sticking to their clothes. Something sharp jabbed Oliver's back, and his wounds were bleeding again.

Percy appeared above them, holding a huge stick. She whacked it down on Acton's back. The man let out a roar.

Oliver got one knee beneath him. Acton rolled and pulled out a pistol. He aimed it at Oliver's chest.

Oliver jammed his arms against the man's arm, straining to push the gun upward.

Then Percy jumped on Acton, ramming her fingers into the man's eyes.

Acton let out a high scream.

"That's for Roberto, asshole." She pushed harder. "And for stabbing Oliver."

Oliver managed to get the gun pushed up above their heads. Acton thrashed wildly and the three of them rolled. Oliver felt empty space under one shoulder and turned his head.

His blood turned to ice. They were right at the edge of the cliff. He got a glimpse of the river down below. Far below. *Shit*.

One more push and they'd all tip over the edge.

"Percy!"

She turned, saw the cliff, and her eyes widened. With a lunge, she reached for the emerald in Acton's hand.

"No!" Acton struggled.

Oliver pulled back and saw Acton's lower body slide over the cliff. His eyes went wide, the whites of his eyes showing.

"Help me." He thrashed, one hand grabbing at Percy, the other hand scrabbling for a hold on the cliff edge.

"Percy, get back—" Oliver yelled.

Acton pulled her over the edge. She grabbed the ledge with one hand, stopping her fall. She hung there, still linked to Acton where they both clutched the emerald. He was holding onto the edge with his other hand, his knuckles white.

Cursing, Oliver grabbed a nearby vine. He tested it, and when it held, he moved closer to the edge. He had to get Percy.

She yanked, pulling the emerald away from Acton. "This is *not* yours."

"You'll never stop us," Acton screamed. "There are others in my organization."

Oliver managed to get a grip on the collar of Percy's shirt. He twisted it, holding on hard.

Acton swung at Percy, trying to dislodge her hold on the emerald or knock her loose. Oliver couldn't tell. She swung wildly and kicked at him.

Then the man lost his grip on the ledge and fell with a scream.

He kicked and flailed all the way down, hitting the

water below with a splash. A moment later, several dark shapes slid off the banks.

"Oh, God," Percy murmured.

Oliver shook his head. "Don't look." It was hard to feel sorry for the man, but it was a horrible way to go.

Then Oliver felt Percy's shirt start to slide through his grip. His heart knocked against his ribs. "Percy, you need to climb back up."

She looked up at him, her gray eyes solemn. Their gazes locked.

He sucked in a breath. There was such sadness on her face.

"Percy—"

"You can do much better than me, Oliver."

He gritted his teeth. "I can do better than a feisty, spirited, intelligent woman? One who lights me up and makes me feel alive?"

She squeezed her eyes closed. "You're not making this easy. I'm doing this for you."

"You seriously thought I'd make it easy for you to leave me?" Oliver shook his head. "I told you, I'm falling for you, Percy. I want to make a life with you. Marriage, kids, house, the whole shebang."

Her eyes widened. "You can't be serious."

"Deadly."

"Why?" She looked at him with such naked longing on her face that it broke his heart.

"Because I'm falling in love with you, and you're falling in love with me, too."

Her face spasmed. "I come from two people who

can't settle down. A thief and a traveler. That's my blood."

"Bullshit. We aren't the people we come from. We're the decisions we make, the actions we take. It's your choice who you are, Percy. What you make of yourself."

Damn, he could feel her shirt slipping farther through his fingers.

Her gaze traced his face. "You're a handsome devil, Oliver Ward. And you need to learn that people will always betray you."

He was losing her. She was right there in front of him, but slipping from his grasp in more ways than one. He dragged in a breath. He always knew that taming Persephone Blake's heart was going to be a tough war. But he was in for the long haul, no matter how much each battle hurt.

"I trust you, Percy. And I'm going to love you, no matter what. I'll be waiting for you."

They stared at each other for another long moment, her fingers clenched on the Emerald Tear.

Then she pressed her boots to the rock wall and pushed. She broke out of his grasp and arched back out into the air, as graceful as a diver.

Then she arrowed down to the river below.

Oliver stayed where he was, clenching the vines. He saw her hit the water, then swim fast toward the far bank. He watched her pull herself out and disappear into the jungle, and fought back the pain in his heart.

I'll be waiting, Percy.

OLIVER OPENED the door to his condo and flicked on the lights.

He sighed. He was tired and hungry, and had spent the day at the university lecturing on the Rio Napo mine.

Every time he talked about it, he thought of Percy and their adventure in the jungle.

A month had passed since he'd returned from Ecuador. Four weeks without her. Hell, he'd been without her longer than he'd known her.

And yet, he thought of her every day.

He dumped his bag on the floor in the entry. He knew his parents were worried. His mother kept inviting him over for dinner, multiple times a week, and the last time, there was the pretty, well-dressed daughter of a friend who'd joined them.

Oliver scrubbed his hands over his face. He was starting to wonder if he'd misjudged things with Percy. Maybe she didn't feel the same way he did? His fingers curled into a fist. What would he do if he never saw her again? The sharp pain in his chest hurt like hell.

Then he froze. A lamp was on in his living room.

He hadn't left any lights on.

He walked in and the gleam of something green shone on his coffee table. His chest tightened. The Emerald Tear rested on the smooth wood.

Scanning the room, he ignored the jewel. He didn't give a damn about the emerald. Percy stepped out of the shadows at the edge of the room.

She looked tired, but still vibrant and brilliantly alive.

Everything in him roared to life, pushing his own weariness aside.

"You think you're so smart, don't you?" she said.

"Hello, Percy."

She threw her arms out. "You planned this! You made me miss you. Every hour of every damn day."

Elation filled him. Persephone Blake had missed him. "Is that what happened?"

She strode closer, determination etched on her face. "I'm not going to let you go now. I'm not going to let you find some silk-suited, coiffed, professor's wife. You lost the chance." She fisted a hand in his shirt and pulled him closer. "You're mine, now."

"I love you, Persephone."

"God help us, I think I love you, too."

And then her sweet mouth was pressed to his. He wrapped his arms around her, pulling her up on her toes and kissing her hard. He was so hungry for her.

Her hands tangled in his hair and she moaned into his mouth.

He nipped her lip. "Missed you." He moved his mouth down her neck, backing her toward his bedroom.

"I missed you, too," she said. "You know I'll drive you crazy. We'll fight and argue."

He smiled. "I can't wait."

Then they were tearing each other's clothes off, and falling onto his bed.

"Wait," he said. "I have something for you." He reached out, grabbing what had been resting on his bedside table from the first day he'd arrived back in Denver.

As she stared at the ring on his palm, her jaw dropped. "You don't do slow, do you, professor?"

"It's not an emerald from Ecuador," he said. "But it's wild and vibrant, like you."

She stared at the oval emerald surrounded by diamonds, then her gaze met his. "You're sure this is what you want?"

"Yes." He lifted her left hand. "A hundred times yes, Percy." He slid the ring on her finger. "You're going to be my greatest adventure."

"God, I love you." Her eyes glimmered with tears, but she was smiling.

Then her mouth was on his again and there were only moans and sighs.

ONE YEAR later

"Where are you taking me, Ward?" Persephone asked. God, the curiosity was killing her. He'd been acting weird all day.

Oliver pulled the car into a parking space between two others on the residential Denver street.

He smiled at her. "I have a surprise for you."

God, a year later and he was still the most beautiful man she knew. A year later, and she was completely in love with the man who was now her husband.

His parents had hidden their initial dismay pretty well when he'd first introduced her to them. But they'd slowly warmed to her, especially when they'd seen that Oliver was happy. Besides, Persephone was darn good at making the Wards laugh—deep, belly laughs for Mr. Ward, and polite tinkling titters from Mrs. Ward. They weren't as stuffy as Persephone had feared. And Oliver's brother Isaac was awesome.

At first, Oliver and Persephone's relationship had scandalized the university. When a university bigwig had politely warned Oliver that marrying an infamous treasure hunter would jeopardize his career, he'd threatened to quit.

"If it's my job or my wife, the university loses," he told them. "Every time."

God, her man. She climbed out of the car, still unable to believe he was hers and that life was so good.

They'd been back in Ecuador several times to help with the dig at the mine site. She'd been a special consultant on the expedition. She winced. Persephone Blake—now Ward—special consultant. She'd never admit just how much she'd enjoyed helping the archeologists.

Oliver had also accompanied her on a few treasure hunts as well, although he preferred to call them artifact acquisition trips. All he'd asked was that she sold the artifacts to reputable dealers and museums.

She smiled. Yes, life was sweet. She fiddled with her emerald ring and wedding band on her finger. And things were about to get more interesting when she finally found the courage to tell him her secret.

He took her hand and pulled her to stand in front of a beautiful Victorian house. She gasped. It was incredibly similar to the picture of the house she'd carried around for years. It was made from warm, red brick, with lots of decorative trim, and it even had a turret.

"What do you think?" he asked.

Bemused, she looked at him. "It's gorgeous." But one

thing Oliver had taught her over the last year was that home wasn't about the walls you lived within.

"It's ours," he said.

She went still. "Say again?"

"Ours. I bought it. It's our new home."

Her mouth dropped open and shockingly, she felt tears well. "Really?"

He cupped her cheeks. "Really. When we aren't traveling, this will be home."

She cleared her throat. "How many bedrooms does it have?"

"Five." He tilted his head. "Why?"

She grabbed his hand and pressed it to her belly. "Because we'll have an extra occupant in about seven months."

His blue eyes flared, and then he was kissing her. Before she could say anything, he dropped to his knees right there on the path, and spread both hands over her belly. The look of wonder on his face made her breath catch.

"A baby?" He looked up. "I want four."

Four. Her brain went blank. That was *insane.* "Two."

"Four."

"I'm not giving birth four times."

"Three."

She huffed out a breath. "We'll see."

"I love you, Percy Ward." He shot her that gorgeous smile that still took away her ability to think. "My life is better with you in it."

"And you're my best adventure, Oliver Ward."

He rose and kissed her in front of the house that

would be their home, and the home of the family they'd make together.

I HOPE you enjoyed Oliver and Percy's story! Read on for *The Emerald Butterfly* featuring ex-SEAL Diego Torres and DEA agent Sloan McBride on the action-packed hunt for the Emerald Butterfly.

THE EMERALD BUTTERFLY

Anna Hackett

CHAPTER ONE

H e stepped out onto the deck and pulled in a deep breath of sea air. It filled him like a drug, racing through his veins. The Florida sun was warm on Diego Torres' skin, and since he was on vacation for the next two weeks, he was a happy man.

Smiling, he crossed the deck of his ship. Pride filled him. The *Storm Nymph* was all his. Well, his and the bank's—he had the mortgage to prove it.

She was a research and salvage vessel. Not the biggest ship out there, but to him she was perfect. He hadn't wanted something that needed a huge crew. The *Nymph* had a large working deck, with an A-frame crane at the back for heavy lifting. A secondary crane was tucked away, one that was used for lifting his collection of ROVs into the water. The remotely operated underwater vehicles were all tucked securely into racks and locked down. Another rack contained scuba tanks, and other

93

compartments were filled with wet suits, buoyancy control device jackets, masks, and fins.

Diego swiveled. The cabins sat belowdecks, and on the main level, he had research labs that would make any scientist happy. There was also a tidy galley and dining room, and the topmost level, ringed by a balcony, contained his bridge. The roof of the bridge bristled with the antennae that made up his high-tech communications systems.

And it was all his. The *Nymph* was the only woman he needed. He crossed the deck to check on some of the gear he wanted to repair and replace over the next few weeks. His crew—a father and son team—were also on vacation, and had gone hunting for a few weeks. Diego was blissfully alone.

He planned to sleep late, do some maintenance jobs on the *Nymph*, drink Coronas while he watched the sunsets, and dodge his nosy family for as long as he could. If his mama or one of his siblings found out he was docked in the harbor, they'd pester him relentlessly. *Come for dinner,* cariño. *Meet my friend's lovely daughter,* mi hijo. *Talk to me,* mi hermano.

Diego loved them, but in the two years since he'd left the Navy, they'd honed pestering into a fine art.

He glanced down at the scars on his arm. His family didn't understand. Didn't have the first clue about the things he'd done and seen, and the friends he'd lost.

Dragging in a breath, he set his hands on his hips. He knew he'd never forget and would never be the man he'd been before. He wanted to shield his family from that.

Protecting his family, his country—that was the reason he'd signed up to be a SEAL in the first place.

His cell phone vibrated in his pocket. For a moment, he considered ignoring it, but then he flicked it open. "Torres."

"Diego. Thank God, I got you."

He recognized the female voice instantly. Darcy Ward, co-owner of Treasure Hunter Security along with her brothers. Declan and Cal were former SEAL buddies of Diego's. He often did work with THS and their clients when it involved underwater expeditions.

"Hey, Darcy."

"I've got a job for you," she said.

He frowned. "I—"

"I know, I know, I'm disrupting your time off," she hurried on. Darcy's energy vibrated through the line. He suspected she was sitting behind her beloved computers. She was especially energetic when she had her fingers on a keyboard. "I wouldn't be calling if it wasn't important."

Diego heard a deep voice rumble in the background.

"Hang on a sec." Darcy's voice turned muffled, like she was covering the phone. "I'm on the phone." A pause. "None of your business." Another pause, and then a huff of breath. "Keep your socks on, I just need a few minutes. I'm working *with* you, not *for* you. I didn't sign a contract to be your slave." Pause. "I'll be there in a *minute*. Diego? I'm back."

"You okay?"

She let out a hiss. "I'm working on a job in DC. An arrogant and annoying job."

"Okay. Look, Darce—"

"Right." She barreled over him. "Where was I? I have a friend. A close friend from college. Her grandfather is dying of cancer and doesn't have long left."

Diego frowned. What the hell did this have to do with him? "That sucks."

"It does, especially since he's all the family she has left. When her parents died, her grandfather took her in. He worked with my dad years ago. Ben was my dad's mentor, and all his life, Ben's been searching for an Incan jewel called the Emerald Butterfly. Have you heard of it?"

"Some lost emerald," Diego said. "Didn't your parents find one like it?"

"They did." Darcy's voice softened. "Mom and Dad met in Ecuador on a treasure hunt to find the Emerald Tear."

Diego was well aware that the feisty Persephone Ward had been an infamous treasure hunter, and Oliver Ward had been an up-and-coming archeologist. They'd collided in the Ecuadorian jungle, and discovered a lost Incan emerald mine and a famous jewel.

"While they were down there, they found evidence of a second giant emerald called the Emerald Butterfly," Darcy continued. "Ben looked for it for years. All the stories said that it had been taken by the Spanish. He found evidence that it was aboard a galleon that was bound for Spain."

Diego felt the hairs rise on the back of his neck. "What ship?"

"The *Nuestra Señora de Atocha*."

Diego sat down on the steps leading up to the bridge.

"Darcy, you know that treasure hunters found the wreck of the *Atocha* in 1985. You can see the artifacts in a museum right here in Key West."

"Diego, we both know that the treasure hunters only found half of the *Atocha*. They never found the sterncastle. The back of the ship would have housed the captain's cabin, where the most valuable items, like a giant emerald, would have been stored for safekeeping. It's still out there, somewhere, unidentified and waiting to be found."

"People have searched for the *Atocha's* sterncastle for decades. No one's found it."

"My friend thinks she has. She wants her grandfather to hold the Emerald Butterfly before he dies."

Diego closed his eyes. *Hell.* His plans for late mornings and drinking beer were rapidly evaporating.

"She needs a ship and someone to help her bring up the emerald."

"Darcy—"

"There's an extra bonus in it for you." Her voice turned cajoling. "Enough for you to buy more equipment for your ship. I know you've had your eye on some fancy diving gear. Those rebreather units, and the full-face masks with the underwater radio-communications system."

"You're mean."

She laughed. "I just like getting my own way. The best thing is that the wreck is right off Key West. You don't have to venture very far, and it might only take a few days." Darcy's tone turned pleading. "Please."

"Why can't someone from THS help her out?"

"Dec's with me here in DC." Her voice turned serious. "We're working on a plan to trap Silk Road."

Diego's blood ran cold. Silk Road—a black-market antiquities ring—was dangerous. "Alone?"

Darcy snorted. "Unfortunately, no. We're working with the FBI." She said the acronym like she'd just admitted to catching an infectious disease. "Cal, Logan, and the others are in Mexico working on a dig. Ronin is off with Peri on an Arctic holiday." Darcy made a sound. "Who goes to the Arctic for a vacation? Anyway, my friend needs help. And I want someone I can trust."

Diego blew out a breath. "Fine. I'll do it."

"Yay! I'm so grateful, Diego. Especially since she'll be coming up your gangplank any second now."

He scowled, raising his head. "You're pretty sure of yourself, aren't you?"

"I'm good." There was amusement in Darcy's tone now. "Now, can I please ask you to be nice?"

Nice? Why would Darcy think he'd be an asshole to a stranger...? *Wait.* "Darcy." He drawled her name as he stood.

"She needs your help. She has a dying grandfather."

"And she's a fucking smart-ass DEA agent. The last time I saw her, she boarded my ship and slapped handcuffs on me!"

"It was all a misunderstanding! You wouldn't let her board, and she had a job to do."

"I don't run drugs."

"They were searching every ship in the marina, Diego. All just a misunderstanding. Be nice." Darcy hung up.

He scanned the docks, glimpsing a few people. His gaze swept over several people heading in his direction, before it zoomed in on a woman walking with a commanding stride along the floating walkway. Cuffed, navy-blue shorts showed off long legs, and a white T-shirt clung to full breasts. A long fall of chestnut-brown hair was loose and a slim backpack rested on one shoulder.

This time there was no pantsuit, tight braid, or tactical vest with DEA emblazoned on it.

Nope, Agent Sloan McBride looked almost normal. She moved with an efficient, energetic stride that told everyone she could handle herself.

As she got closer, her gaze flicked up and met his. She was still too far away for him to see the color of her eyes.

But he remembered. They were gray-green and framed by dark lashes.

"Damn you, Darcy," he muttered to himself.

* * *

SLOAN MCBRIDE STRODE up the ramp to the ship.

Diego Torres didn't look pleased to see her.

But she was a woman who worked in a male-domi-nated profession, and she'd never let a scowling, rugged face deter her before. Even one as mouthwatering as Diego's. He wasn't classically handsome—his nose had been broken before, and his cheeks were covered in sexy stubble. But perfect had never been that attractive to Sloan.

"Hi." She stuck her hands in her pockets. "Darcy tell you I was coming?"

He slid his cell phone into the pocket of his faded denim shorts. "About one minute ago."

Ouch. His voice was several degrees colder than the water lapping at the hull of the ship. *Thanks, Darce.*

"I need your help," Sloan said.

"Planning to slap some handcuffs on me and order me around to get your way?"

The mention of handcuffs made her belly flutter. The last time she'd seen Diego, she'd been in a hurry to stop a large drug shipment from leaving Miami. Maybe if she'd explained things better, things would've gone a lot smoother with Diego Torres. But at the time, she'd been running on coffee and no sleep, and under a tight deadline.

"Sorry, I left my cuffs at home this time."

Dark, silky eyes stared back at her, and an image slammed into her head. For a brilliant second, she imagined what it would be like to have six-feet-plus of hard muscle covered in smooth, brown skin under her, cuffed and at her mercy.

God. A hot flush raced over her skin, and she cleared her throat. She wasn't here for that. She had a job to do, a very personal one.

She tucked some hair behind her ear. "I'm on a leave of absence from work."

"Well, wish I could tell you that it was a pleasure to see you again." His scowl deepened.

Double ouch. "Look, I was in a rush last time we met. I was running on fumes and no sleep, and in the middle of a really big operation. You were not being helpful, and things were time sensitive—"

"You boarded my ship without a good explanation. Nor did you—"

"I had a warrant."

"You could have explained."

"I didn't have time," she snapped. "Sixteen-hundred pounds of cocaine were headed out on a ship, and I needed to stop it. You didn't need to be an asshole."

He tilted his head and crossed his arms over his broad chest. She watched those muscled arms flex, and remembered that he'd been a Navy SEAL. He had not gone soft since he'd left the Navy.

She blew out a breath. "I'm sorry, all right? I really need your help."

He was quiet for a beat, and then he leaned against the railing. She took a second to look over the deck of his ship. Everything was neat and tidy, the deck was clean, and there were stacks of all kinds of equipment, half of which she didn't recognize.

"You're after an emerald," he said.

Sloan nodded. "My granddad has been trying to find it for over three decades."

"He's sick."

Pain shot through her. "Cancer. He's put up a good fight for three years, but he's not going to win." Her grief stole her breath.

"I'm sorry."

Diego's quiet, sincere words hit her. "Thank you. I want to do this for him, and let him hold the gem before he..." It was unbearable to think of her world without her granddad in it.

"Treasure hunters already salvaged the front half of

the *Atocha*, and lots of people have tried to find the missing part of the ship. What makes you think you can find it?"

"Because I'm a genius."

His lips quirked. "Modest, too."

She smiled. "I don't play games, Mr. Torres. And you already know I detest wasting time."

"Right. So, tell me how you plan to find it?"

"I minored in computer science at college. That's how I met Darcy."

"So, you're a computer whiz, too."

"Yes. I've been working on a program to simulate weather patterns, storms, ocean currents. The *Nuestra Señora de Atocha* and another ship with it, the *Santa Margarita*, sank in a hurricane off the Keys in 1622. Spain attempted to recover what they could and found over half of the *Margarita's* cargo. But the *Atocha* went down in deeper water, and another hurricane swept in about a month later and scattered the wreckage even farther."

"And you think after all this time, that a fancy computer program will find her?"

Sloan smiled. "Yes. I've been plugging in simulations of the weather, how the ship likely broke up, the effects of the second hurricane."

His gaze sharpened. "You really know where the missing part of the ship is."

"I do. And I'd like your help to locate it and bring the emerald up."

His dark gaze moved over her face and she stared

right back at him. He was so damn attractive. Damn her for having a weakness for rugged men.

Diego reached up and stroked his stubbled chin. "Why do I feel like there's a catch?"

Perceptive man. She wasn't surprised. She'd seen his service records, knew he'd been a hell of a SEAL. And now he ran a successful business. There were brains behind the brawn.

"My apartment here in Miami was ransacked. They didn't get my computer program, but they took all my notes on the *Atocha*. All my data, and everything about the emerald."

He cursed. "Silk Road?"

"Darcy and her brothers think so. The Emerald Butterfly is something that would attract them. I'm pretty sure they'll be right on my heels."

Diego cursed again, his gaze moving over her shoulder. "You said you left the handcuffs at home. Did you leave your handgun, too?"

She frowned. "No." She had her personal Glock holstered at the small of her back.

"Good." He pulled a massive Desert Eagle handgun from the back of his shorts.

Her eyes widened. "You want to shoot me for suggesting we work together? Seems a bit excessive, Torres."

He threw her a look. "Two big guys are heading this way. Both armed."

Coolness ran over Sloan, and she dropped her backpack and smoothly drew her Glock from the back of her shorts. She stepped up beside Diego and turned. "Why didn't you say so?"

"I just did." He sounded unhappy.

She rolled her eyes. "Can we save the banter for after, and just take care of these guys?"

CHAPTER TWO

D iego crouched by the railing. "They've split up."
He couldn't see where the men had gone. They
were using the other docked boats for cover.

"Plan?" Sloan's tone was cool and even.

He scanned the deck. "Let's face these fuckers
head-on."

She rolled her eyes. "Big, bad SEALs can't be subtle,
can they? You just rush in with guns blazing."

He narrowed his gaze. "You have a better idea?
Maybe flash your badge at them and ask them nicely to
put their guns down?"

"You are so annoying."

"Right back at you, McBride."

"It's Sloan." She looked over his ship. "And I do have
an idea. We take up positions on the other side of your
deck and let them come aboard. Lure them right in and
then take them down."

Diego considered it. "Okay. But if you get my ship

shot up, I'm getting payback." He wrapped a hand around her arm and pulled her across the deck. He circled racks of diving equipment.

"I'll pay for any damages," she said.

"Oh, you'll pay. But I won't make you pay with money."

She frowned. "What the hell does that mean?"

He smiled, but then he saw a flash of movement at the ramp and he waved his hand. They ducked down behind the racks. Sloan's body brushed his. She didn't fidget, just moved into position, gun aimed and gaze steady.

"Here they come." Diego focused, feeling his usual pre-combat calm wash over him. The two big bruisers came up the ramp, both holding handguns.

They fanned out, cautiously crossing the deck.

"Ready?" Diego murmured.

"Oh, yeah." Then she raised her voice. "Gentlemen? Are you following me?"

The men froze in place, then crouched.

"We want to know the location of the shipwreck," one of the men called out.

"Let me guess," Sloan said. "You're Silk Road."

"Just give us the coordinates and we won't hurt you."

Sloan snorted. "Can you believe these guys?" She looked pissed and insulted.

"Nope," Diego said.

She raised her voice again. "Do you guys know what I do for a living?"

Diego watched the goons through the gap in the

storage rack. He saw the men share a confused look. *Idiots.* You never went in without all the intel.

Sloan shook her head. "You didn't do your research. That's lazy."

The men looked angry now, the larger guy's face becoming mottled.

"There's only one of you," the big guy bit out, "and two of us."

Diego looked at the deck. *Really big idiots.*

"I'm done." Sloan popped up and fired.

The gun flew out of Goon One's hand. He cried out and stumbled backward.

Goon Two dove and fired, bullets pinging off metal.

They were hitting his ship. *Assholes.* Diego rose, firing at the same time Sloan did.

"I'll keep them pinned and you circle around." She didn't even look at him as she issued her orders.

He nodded, moving quietly, and ducking behind some equipment. He knew every inch of his deck intimately, and the Navy had trained him very well at sneaking around. He made his way closer to the two men.

They were both firing in Sloan's direction. He hoped to hell she stayed in cover. Crouching, he stopped, eyeing the patch of open deck he needed to cross to reach the Silk Road men.

Suddenly, the men straightened and turned away from his location. Diego swiveled his head and saw that Sloan was out in the open, purposely drawing their attention. *The little fool.*

That's when he spotted movement behind Sloan. A *third* man, creeping closer to her.

Shit.

Diego pivoted and ran. He powered across the deck toward Sloan. He heard the men cursing, and more weapons fire. Sloan stared at him, anger in her gaze. He raised his gun, firing at the shape over Sloan's shoulder.

The man yelled and Diego slammed into Sloan. He spun midair, turning so he was on the bottom. They hit the deck, sliding in behind some crates.

"Fuck, Torres. You're ruining the plan."

"Third assailant."

"I saw him," she said, voice sharp. "You didn't have to rescue me so dramatically. Do I look like a clueless civilian to you?"

Diego rolled to his knees, and Sloan did the same. They both came up firing. "*Dios*, you're busting my balls in the middle of a firefight! For stopping you getting a bullet."

She snorted. "I was hardly going to get hit." She paused to fire. "And I have no interest in your balls, Torres."

He fired again. "Really?"

"Really. Cover me."

She leaped over the crate, and he cursed. He rose and fired again.

She strode out like some badass warrior queen. She hit one goon in the arm, and he spun away with a shout. Next, she landed a hard kick into the second man's midsection. He slammed into the railing.

Where was the third one? Diego spotted a flash of black. He pressed one palm to the crate and leaped over. He charged at the man, his face grim.

The goon's blue eyes widened. He fumbled to get his gun up, but Diego calmly raised his weapon and fired. The man jerked, just as Diego felt a sharp burn on his arm where a bullet grazed him.

Diego tackled the man to the deck. With two vicious punches, the man's eyes rolled back in his head, and he slumped down, unconscious.

"Torres! Watch out."

At Sloan's shout, he swiveled. The first man, covered in blood, stood with a large knife clutched in his hand. He bared his teeth.

"Really?" Diego shook his head and walked steadily toward the man. The man lunged and Diego dodged. It had been a while since he'd been in a good knife fight. He grinned.

The man looked at his grin and frowned. Diego bent his knees, ready for the man's next move.

Suddenly, a lean body pushed into Diego, knocking him out of the way. He watched Sloan kick the man, knocking the knife out of his hand. She jumped up, landing a vicious roundhouse kick to the man's head.

The man fell like a sack of bricks. He clutched his head, writhing on the deck, groaning.

Sloan kicked the knife away, and then yanked something out of her pocket. He realized it was a plastic zip tie. She leaned down and tied the man's hands together.

"What the hell?" Diego snapped. "I had it under control."

Gray-green eyes flashed at him. "Just stopping you from getting a nasty slash." She shot him a smug smile. "I *am* in law enforcement, and you're an innocent civilian."

He grunted. *Dios*, she was a ball-buster. And exceptional in a fight. He could watch her fight all day long.

She turned, clearly searching for the other two men. Diego spotted the two goons disappearing down the gangplank, one leaning heavily on the other.

Diego moved toward them, but Sloan shook her head. "Let them go. I'll make a call, and have someone come and pick up this idiot." She toed the man at her feet.

Then her gaze zeroed in on Diego's arm. "Is that your blood?"

He looked at the sleeve of his battered T-shirt. "It's minor."

"Get inside and get your first aid kit. Let me see it."

Dios, more orders. "It's nothing—"

"Now, Torres." She strode up the steps leading into the dining room and galley. "I need you all in one piece for this treasure hunt."

He watched her ass and long legs as she moved ahead of him. Damn, for once he was happy to follow her orders.

SLOAN FELT HYPED up from the fight. Adrenaline ran rampant through her system.

Some agent friends had stopped by and carted off the sullen Silk Road man, and the skirmish had left her even more eager to find the Emerald Butterfly.

She'd recovered her backpack and entered the galley. Instantly, she spotted Diego sitting at a table, a towel wrapped around his arm. Her gaze hit his bloody shirt and her stomach rolled. At least it looked like the bleeding had stopped. An industrial-sized first aid kit rested on the table.

Then she looked at the magnificent painting on the wall and sucked in a breath.

He looked over his shoulder. "It's called *The Cave of the Storm Nymphs*. Done by a British painter, Poynter."

"It's amazing." It was a dramatic image, with three beautiful, naked nymphs lolling on their treasure in a cave, while a sinking ship floundered outside in the waves.

"It caught my eye." His dark gaze burned into her. "Apparently I have a thing for bloodthirsty women."

She made her way over and opened the first aid kit. She fished around and found it was well-stocked.

"Shirt off," she ordered.

For once, he did as she asked without talking back. His face was composed, and if he was in pain, he wasn't showing it.

He gripped the back of the shirt with one hand and yanked it over his head. Sloan froze.

Holy. Hell. The man was pure, solid muscle. His chest was like marble slabs with hard pecs, and a ridged, six-pack abdomen. She saw a faint trail of dark hair leading down into his shorts. His skin was all sleek and brown, with no white tan lines. She guessed he had genetics to thank for that.

Her gaze fell on the intricate black ink that covered his left shoulder, bicep and pec. She'd never had a thing for tattoos before, but Diego wore his well. So well. She peered closely at the markings. They looked like Aztec designs to her, but she was no expert.

Her gaze traveled over him, drinking him all in, and then fell on his right arm. There was no sleek skin here. His forearm was covered in terrible scars. Some sort of knife wound, it appeared. God, whatever had been done to him had to have been agony.

Her gaze moved back up, and she saw the bloody crease in his bicep. The bullet had just winged him, thank God. She stared at the bright-red blood smeared over his skin, and her stomach did a slow, sickening somersault.

Ugh. She hated her little weakness. One she hid ruthlessly from her colleagues. If she didn't look directly at the blood, she was usually fine. No way she was fainting in front of Diego Torres.

She grabbed some antiseptic wipes from the kit, tore them open, and started cleaning his injury.

"What's wrong?" Diego asked.

She flicked her gaze up to his. "Nothing."

"You've gone pale." He glanced down at his arm. "It isn't that bad. I'm sure you've seen worse."

She nodded. The wipe she was using had turned red, and she tasted bile in her throat. Tossing it down, she grabbed a fresh one. Doggedly, she went back to wiping his wound. "It doesn't need stitches."

Suddenly, a big, scarred hand pressed over hers. "It's fine." He tilted his head, a shit-eating grin lighting up his face. "You don't like blood."

"No one likes blood." Damn, her voice was too fast, pitched a little too high.

"You look like you're about to faint."

She gritted her teeth. "Am not."

He shook his head. "Tough, rock-hard Agent McBride has a weakness." Diego reached into the first aid kit, pulled out a large adhesive bandage and slapped it over his wound.

Instantly, Sloan's belly calmed. "I do not."

He snorted, and she decided it was time to change the subject. She looked at his tattoo again.

Diego saw the direction of her gaze. "I got it a year after I became a SEAL. Was on leave in Mexico. The Aztec designs seemed appropriate."

"Your family's Mexican-American?"

He nodded. "Not that my ma was impressed with the ink, but she ignores it, now."

"It's amazing." Before she realized what she was doing, she reached out and stroked the design on his shoulder. She'd been right, his skin was smooth.

Electricity arced between them, and she sucked in a breath. Their eyes met.

Liquid heat moved through Sloan. His eyes looked like velvet, sucking her in. Her fingers brushed against his tattoo again.

"Thanks for bandaging my injury." Diego's voice was husky.

"You bandaged it, I just swiped at it." She wasn't mentioning the blood.

"Yeah, but it's nice to have someone take care of it other than myself. Once, I had to stitch myself up on a mission in Afghanistan." He grimaced. "Not fun."

She imagined him in some hot desert camp, hunkered

down and gritting his teeth through the pain as he stuck a needle through his skin. Without thinking, she leaned forward and pressed a kiss to the bandage.

Diego groaned. "Hell, Sloan."

She leaned back and pulled in a breath. "We don't like each other."

"I like you. You just pissed me off when you boarded my ship with a team of DEA agents."

"And handcuffed you," she reminded him.

He shrugged a shoulder. "I didn't mind that bit so much."

Heat hit her belly in a rush. His hand curled around her arm and tugged her forward until their faces were a whisper apart.

"Kiss me," he murmured.

"Don't tell me what to do."

He made a growling sound, but she slid a hand around his neck and leaned forward. Their lips met.

Oh, his lips were firm but full. She opened her mouth and instantly his tongue slid inside.

As though it were a signal, they devoured each other. Sloan shifted, and practically sat in his lap. He groaned, and her own moan vibrated through her. The man kissed rough, hard, and real. And he tasted even better than she'd dreamed.

After a long moment they pulled apart, and Sloan's brain refused to form any thoughts. "Well."

Diego smiled and her gaze fell to his lips. Lips she'd tasted and knew the feel of.

"I was gonna say, wow," he said.

Wow worked for her, too.

"I'll help you find your wreck and the Emerald Butterfly," he said.

Sloan closed her eyes, then opened them. "Thank you." She cleared her throat. "But no more kisses, though."

"We'll see."

She frowned. "Torres, I'm serious."

He smiled a slow, sexy grin. "How are you going to stop yourself from kissing me?"

So arrogant. Time to focus on their treasure hunt. "Do you want to see what I've got?"

When his smile widened, she realized how that had sounded. "My research. See my research on the *Atocha*."

"Sure thing." He stood and pulled his shirt back on.

The wicked part of Sloan moaned in disappointment. *Down, hussy.* He nodded toward the bridge, and she followed him up the stairs.

As they entered the uppermost level of the *Storm Nymph*, Sloan looked around with interest. All the high-tech consoles and screens gleamed. She knew he looked perfect out on the deck, with the sea breeze ruffling his dark hair, but this suited him too. As he moved to a console, she could see him as the captain of a pirate ship, striding across the deck, barking orders, seducing virgins.

God. She needed to get a grip. She pulled out her tablet from her backpack and set it down on a table that was covered in paper maps.

"Let me show you my weather program." She pulled it up. Electronic maps flashed on the screen.

Diego crossed his muscled arms, studying her research.

"The sterncastle of the *Atocha* is about forty miles off Key West."

"That's a long way from where the other half of the ship was found."

She nodded. "That's why no one's found it. The hurricane caused it to drift a long way before she sank, and the second hurricane moved it even farther away."

"This is your show, Sloan. Once we get out there, we'll know."

She smiled. "That's right, I'm the boss."

He arched a brow and shot her a heated look. "*Chiquita*, it's my ship. There's only one Captain."

That look made her insides quiver. "When can we leave?"

"I need to stock up on some things so we can leave in the morning. Grab your gear from your car, and I'll show you to your cabin."

Excitement winged through her. She thought of her granddad, lying so still and sick in a hospital bed. "We're going to do this."

"Yeah," Diego said. "We're going to find ourselves a priceless emerald."

She held out her hand for a businesslike handshake. His big hand engulfed hers, and electricity zipped along her arm. A smile tipped up the corner of his lips.

Sloan hoped to hell she wasn't in over her head.

CHAPTER THREE

The boat engines vibrated under his feet, and outside, the sun was shining in a clear, blue sky.

Diego maneuvered the *Storm Nymph* out of the marina. He loved this. Loved knowing he was captain of his own ship, and that he got to spend the day out in the sun and fresh air. There, no one would be shooting at him.

Hopefully.

Out the window, Sloan came into view on the deck below. He sucked in a breath. She was wearing short cutoffs—very short—made of faded denim. They showed off long, toned legs. She wore a bikini top in electric blue that lovingly cupped her full breasts. Her thick, brown hair was pulled up in a messy knot on the top of her head.

Shit. He'd fantasized about that glossy hair loose and spread over his pillows. And those legs wrapped around his hips, while he tasted that sweet, sexy mouth again.

And the thing was, he'd been fantasizing about it for months. Ever since she'd first boarded his ship and handcuffed him.

He shook his head. He had a job to focus on, and Silk Road nipping at his ass. That had to be his focus right now, not kissing Sloan McBride senseless.

She disappeared from view, and a moment later, he heard footsteps as she came up to the bridge.

"Hey," she called out. "How long until we reach the location?"

"Couple of hours. Sleep well?"

"No." She leaned against the console. "You?"

"Not so much."

"Not fun when bullets are flying," she said.

He hadn't even given that a thought. His dreams had been full of her. He noticed her eyes were shadowed. "You okay?"

She shrugged a shoulder. "I just spoke with my grandfather."

"He okay?"

"Tired, but hanging in there." She straightened. "I'm really grateful that Darcy, Dec, and Cal's parents go to see him at the hospital all the time."

"It must be hard not to be close to him."

She nodded. "But I know holding the Emerald Butterfly will cheer him up."

As Diego moved the *Nymph* out into open water, he picked up speed. Sloan sat down at the table nearby, working on her research notes and tapping on her tablet. The silence felt companionable. Most women he knew felt compelled to fill any quiet with words. His mama and sisters were champions at it.

The minutes slipped by. A few times, Sloan asked questions, and scribbled in her notes. Then he looked at his screen and realized they'd arrived. He scanned the blue water around them. The sea was calm and empty.

"We're here." He cut the engines. "Let me drop anchor and then we'll get to work."

Once the *Nymph* was secure, Diego turned to face Sloan. His gut clenched. *Dios*, the look on her face. It was excited and energized.

"What's the plan?" she asked.

"Now we get the ROV out." He strode off the bridge and, gripping the railings, hurried down the steps.

"Remotely operated vehicle."

He nodded. "I have a collection of them." He pointed to the rack where the ROVs were stowed. "Larger one has attachments for recovering objects in deep water. But we only need this guy today." He unlocked a smaller, boxy-shaped ROV that was painted bright yellow. "This is Poseidon. He'll relay video feed back to us. Step back."

He grabbed the crane controls and maneuvered the yellow crane arm until the ROV was dangling over the side of the ship. He lowered it into the water.

"Now to the computer control room."

She followed him. "Sounds fancy."

"It's not. I converted a cupboard."

They moved through the dry lab, and he opened the computer room door.

Sloan laughed. "You weren't joking."

The tiny room was dominated by a large chair with joysticks built into the arms. Big screens covered the wall.

Diego dropped into the chair and fired up the system. The screens flickered to life, and Sloan sat close behind him on a stool.

He touched the joysticks and the ROV zoomed away from the *Nymph*, powering through the water.

Sloan leaned over his shoulder, gaze glued to the screen, and intense interest on her face. They watched as a trio of gorgeous blue fish swam past the camera.

"Halfway down," he said. "Visibility is great."

She was leaning against him, and damn, she smelled good. He could smell her fruity shampoo, and a scent that was pure Sloan. He ignored his hardening cock and focused on the screen. The sandy bottom came into view.

"Boy, I want one of these ROVs," she said.

"If we have time, I'll teach you to operate it."

"Really?"

He turned his head and she did the same. They found themselves only an inch apart. His gaze dropped to her lips. "Really."

"I'd like that," she said huskily.

The screen beeped, and he ripped his gaze from hers. He forced himself to concentrate on operating his expensive piece of equipment.

"I'm going to set Poseidon up to run a search grid. If we spot anything of interest, we'll note the coordinates, and check it out when we dive."

"Great."

Her warm breath puffed against his neck. His cock

was pressing hard against his zipper now. *Dios*, what had he done to deserve this torture?

The ROV began sweeping back and forth through the water. They had a clear view of the sandy bottom, dotted with lumps of rocks and coral.

"So, where are you from, Torres?" she asked.

"Right here. Miami."

Her eyebrows rose. "You have family here?"

"A mob of them. My mother, two sisters, and a brother. My dad passed from a heart attack a few years back."

"I'm sorry."

He nodded. His father's death had rocked them all. Diego had been deployed on a classified mission at the time. His papa had already been buried by the time he'd returned home and found out.

"It's hard to lose someone you love."

Her voice was quiet, and he remembered that she'd lost her parents. "Yeah." He cleared his throat. "Don't get me started on all my uncles, aunts, cousins, second cousins."

She stared at him.

"What?"

"You have this whole *lone sea wolf* vibe going on. I got the impression that your ship was your only family, and you sprang fully formed from a clam, or something."

He barked out a laugh, but guilt nipped at him. "I visit my family."

Shrewd eyes watched him until Diego felt naked.

"You know, I interrogate suspects for a living. I can smell a lie a mile away."

He hunched his shoulders.

"You keep a wall up," she said quietly. "You keep your family at bay."

He hunched more. "You sound like the Navy shrinks now. I see my family. They're loud, noisy, and nosy, so I can't be blamed for wanting to avoid them sometimes." He needed to change the subject. "What about your family?"

Pain flashed on her face. "Dead or dying."

God, he was an idiot. "Sloan—"

She shook her head. "It's okay, Diego. My parents were killed in a gas station robbery when I was thirteen. They were killed by an eighteen-year-old addict who was high on drugs. He took twenty dollars from my mom's purse. That's all she had. Twenty dollars. They lost their lives for a twenty."

"*Chiquita*..." Something clicked in his head. "That's why you joined the DEA."

She nodded. "I wanted to stop other kids losing their parents." She smiled, but it was sad. "Luckily, I had my grandfather."

And now she was losing him, too.

"If I had a loud, noisy, nosy family," Sloan said, "I'd never keep them out."

They stared at each other, and he pulled in a breath. "I didn't come back the same man who left." He looked down at the scars on his arm. "I scared them."

Slim fingers touched his shoulder. "I thought SEALs never gave up?"

He wanted to kiss her again. He wanted to forget all

the pain and the darkness that still rotted his insides, and lose himself in Sloan McBride.

But she turned her head and looked at the screen. Her eyes widened. "Hey. What's that?"

Diego glanced over. The ROV was passing over a large, rocky outcrop. Fish darted around like tiny dancers. "Rock with some coral. It's natural."

She sighed. "Let's keep looking."

The ROV continued its sweeps. This was the not-so-glamorous side of underwater archeology. The boring side that required patience.

A few times, Sloan left the room to scan the horizon. "No sign of Silk Road."

But Diego's nerves were tingling. Nerves that had been honed during his time as a SEAL. Silk Road didn't give up, either. Declan and Treasure Hunter Security had taken down two of the group's bigwigs. Only one was left—the so-called Collector.

He'd be consolidating his power, and something like the Emerald Butterfly would be just the kind of artifact that would help him do it.

Diego turned back to the screen. He gently moved the controls, and Poseidon reached the end of the search grid.

There was no sign of the *Atocha*. He turned to Sloan.

"Anything?" she asked.

He shook his head. "Nothing."

SLOAN SAT HUNCHED over her tablet, rerunning her simulations. Beside her rested a plate with a half-eaten sandwich. She'd been so sure her coordinates were right....

"Sloan." Diego appeared beside her. "This kind of hunt takes time and patience. Quit beating yourself up."

"We don't have time." She threw an arm out. "Silk Road is out there waiting to pounce, and granddad—"

The pain was bright and sharp. She was going to lose the man who was most important to her. She'd be alone.

"Sloan?"

Diego's deep voice made her shake off the emotions. Or at least, she tried to. "I think my assumptions on the windspeeds might be off. It puts us a bit too far east."

He looked at her for a moment before he nodded. "Poseidon is charged and ready to go back in the water."

She stood. "Okay then, let's get to work."

As the crane lowered the ROV beneath the waves, Sloan scanned the horizon. There were no other ships in sight. No sign of Silk Road.

But she knew they were out there, somewhere.

Soon, she stood behind Diego's chair in the cramped computer room. The blue light from the screen washed over his rugged face, and he moved the controls with experienced ease. There was so much more to Diego Torres than the angry loner she'd pegged him to be when they'd first clashed.

Dragging her gaze to the screen, she watched the ROV get closer to the sandy seafloor.

"Come here," Diego murmured.

"Excuse me?"

"Here."

She circled his chair. "What do—"

"I'm going to teach you to operate the ROV." He kicked a small stool over in front of his chair.

Her pulse leaped. She sat, and was instantly aware that she was sitting between his legs, surrounded by him. She breathed deep. He smelled like the sea, and she felt her body's response deep in her belly.

He reached over and grabbed her hands, pulling them back so they wrapped around the joysticks. His big, callused hands closed over hers.

"Go easy on the controls," he warned. "Small movements."

She moved her fingers and gasped softly. He was right. The ROV controls were super-responsive. She watched the machine move under her control and smiled. After a few false starts, she got the hang of it.

"That's it." There was a smile in his voice. "You're a natural."

He was so close behind her that she could feel his breath on her neck.

Dammit. She hadn't factored in this. Coming here, she'd known they'd gotten off to a rocky start, and that might make things difficult. But this? This insane, electric attraction? No, she hadn't imagined being desperate to tear Diego Torres' clothes off and explore that rock-hard body of his.

Her last lover had been a nice, well-dressed, assistant district attorney. He'd been fun, but hadn't left her a hot, trembling mess.

Diego's fingers flexed on hers and he leaned forward, his lips brushing the back of her neck.

She shivered. *God.* Sloan's inner hussy started begging.

Diego suddenly stilled, and she risked a glance back over her shoulder. Her gaze locked with deep-brown eyes and her mind went blank.

"Sloan."

Their hands moved as one, bumping the controls. Poseidon turned sharply in the water.

They both hissed out a breath. Together, they righted the underwater vehicle. Then Diego went still once more.

"What?" She frowned. "What's wrong?"

He was staring at the screen. "Look."

She turned to peer at the screen, as well. Sand and coral, mostly. Then she spotted it.

She leaned forward, her heart beating hard. No, it couldn't be. She easily made out the cylindrical shape of a cannon, partly buried in the sand.

Diego took control and moved the ROV closer. A strange clump of something was visible on the sand. She frowned. It looked like a pile of clam shells.

No. It was a clump of coins covered in buildup from the sea. "Diego."

"I see it."

"There's something else." She leaped up, pointing to a dark shape on the sand. "There."

Something green.

Her breath caught in her throat, and Diego zoomed the image in. It wasn't huge, but it was definitely an emerald.

She spun, grinning at him. Unable to stop herself, she

leaned down and smacked a quick kiss to his lips. "We found it. Fancy a dive?"

Hot eyes bored into hers. "Sure."

Energized, Sloan raced out onto the deck. As Diego brought Poseidon back to the boat, she stripped off her clothes and pulled a wet suit on over her bikini. She'd done some recreational diving before, so she knew her gear.

After locking down the ROV, Diego pulled his own suit on, and helped set out gear for them both. Sloan pulled on her weight belt, watching him. Diego looked like he was preparing for a walk around the block, not to scuba dive.

While she might know the diving equipment, he checked it over with the ease of someone who did this every day. She wondered at the missions he'd dived on to help defend his country. He pulled the rest of his own dive gear on, and then hefted a set of tanks. He held them out for her. She let the weight settle on her back, and did up her vest, while he slipped into his own tanks.

At the edge of the deck, she pulled on her fins and mask. Diego gave her a quick refresher on the hand signals, and then with a nod, they both tipped backward into the water.

Silence. An explosion of bubbles rose up around her mask, and she sank into the clear water.

The sound of her own breathing filled her head. Diego shot her the okay sign, and she returned it. Then he tipped his thumb down in the sign to descend.

With a powerful kick, he turned and started toward the bottom. Sloan followed.

God, she remembered why she loved diving. Even with all the gear, she felt a sense of weightlessness. Fish flitted past her. So pretty. Down here, there were no drugs, no douchebags. No suffering. Just bright, vivid life.

Diego led the way, glancing at the bulky dive watch on his wrist a few times. She easily pictured him with a team of SEALs, diving on a mission.

Soon, they reached the bottom. She adjusted her buoyancy control device vest so she hung just above the sand.

Diego pointed ahead, and they swam forward. Then, he grabbed her arm.

She saw what he'd spotted and her breath hitched.

It was definitely an emerald. About the size of her thumb, it was just resting on the sand, as though it were simply waiting to be found.

She moved over it, and then carefully picked it up, holding it in front of her face.

Behind his regulator, she could tell Diego was smiling.

He signaled at her to continue searching. She kicked gently, exploring the sand. As she examined the cannon, movement in the distance caught her eye. A few curious reef sharks. They didn't come closer and eventually darted off.

Then, Diego grabbed her arm, and pulled her to a coral outcrop. He pointed.

She frowned, studying the coral, unable to figure out why Diego thought it was important. She turned to look at him questioningly, and he pointed to the coral once more.

Then, her gaze whipped back, and her chest locked. Coins. Like they'd seen on the screen on the ship, these were other piles of corroded coins. They'd definitely found the rest of the *Atocha*. She knew that the wooden hull would have decayed long ago, but in her head, she could picture it resting here, torn from the rest of the ship, and lost to the sea.

And that meant the Emerald Butterfly was here somewhere, too.

Finally, Diego looked at his watch and pointed upward. She didn't want to leave, but she nodded. They'd be back.

Together, they started their ascent to the surface. The hull of the *Storm Nymph* got larger and larger above them.

As one, they broke the surface of the water.

"My God, Diego," Sloan said as they climbed aboard, smiling like crazy. "We found it!"

On the deck, she spun, holding up the small emerald and laughing.

He took her tanks and set them down. "We sure did." He shed his own gear.

Excitement thrummed through her. They'd found it. She couldn't wait to tell her grandfather. They'd found the rest of the *Atocha*.

And Diego had helped her make it happen.

They grinned at each other, and she watched as Diego pushed his wet hair back off his face.

Sloan leaped on him and slammed her mouth against his.

He grunted as he caught her...and kissed her back.

So. Good. She slid a hand into his hair, her tongue sliding against his. His big hands moved to cup her ass in her wet suit.

Right now, she wasn't sure what felt better—knowing she'd found the *Atocha,* or kissing Diego Torres.

CHAPTER FOUR

esire slammed into Diego like a tidal wave. *Dios*, she tasted so good. Felt so good.

Sloan's tongue tangled with his, and he went to his knees, lowering her to the deck. He covered her body with his and slid his hands into her hair. He gently tugged the damp strands free of their tie.

She wound her arms and legs around him, and moaned into his mouth. That's when a ringing phone broke the silence.

Dammit. He recognized the ring tone and cursed his high-tech comms system.

The phone stopped ringing and he kissed Sloan again, pulling her closer. But the break was minuscule. His cellphone started ringing again.

She pulled back. "You going to answer that?"

He slid a hand down her sleek body, toying with the fastening of her wet suit. "I'd prefer to ignore it." The damn thing started ringing again.

Sloan bit her lip. "Whoever it is, they're persistent."

With a sigh, Diego rose. It hurt to let her go. "Like you wouldn't believe." He moved over to his discarded clothes and snatched up the phone. "*Hola,* Mama."

His mother's voice spilled through the line.

He sighed. "I know, Mama. I took the boat out." He glanced over at Sloan.

She was watching him with undisguised interest.

"No, Ma, I can't come for dinner tonight. I... No. Yes. S*i,* I know I'm a huge disappointment as a son. Get Teresa or Ricardo to give you grandbabies." He waited while his mama went off on her usual "I'll-die-without-any-grandchildren" spiel.

Sloan rose, and his gaze moved over her as she stripped off the wet suit. *Fucking gorgeous.* That tiny blue bikini made his cock surge. He swallowed a groan. No, it wasn't the bikini, it was what was under it.

"Diego? Diego?"

He realized his mother was calling his name. "Sorry, Mama. I didn't catch that."

Sloan glanced back at him, and when she noticed why he was distracted, she laughed. It was full and throaty. *Dios,* he was so hard he hurt.

His mother went silent, which wasn't her natural state. *Shit.*

"Is that a woman's voice I hear, Diego?"

Double shit. "She's a client."

"You're on vacation."

He cursed.

"Language, Diego. That mouth. Who is she? What's her name?"

"Ma."

"Is she pretty?"

"Mama, I'll call you when I get back."

"You'll come for a family dinner?" There was hope in her voice and he closed his eyes. He remembered Sloan's face when she talked about losing her family.

"Yeah, I'll come for dinner."

"You will? *Bueno*! I'll make my chicken tostadas." She paused. "Bring your friend with the nice laugh."

"Bye, Mama."

Sloan now had a towel slung around her hips and was studying the emerald. "So, you *are* close to your family."

"My mother likes to meddle. She finds the time to bug me and all my siblings."

"That's nice," Sloan murmured. "And she wants grandbabies."

Diego groaned. "And she isn't shy about letting us know." He tugged on his T-shirt. "Come on. Let's get that pretty emerald into my safe and then we have a salvage to plan."

After the small emerald was locked up safely, they got to work in the dry lab and he set out the scans the ROV had taken. He and Sloan planned and argued. As they worked, he grabbed some beers and chips.

"You shouldn't avoid your family," she said, interrupting their strategic planning.

He pressed his hands to the bench. "I told you, my time as a SEAL...I saw things. Did things. Lost good friends. Fuck." He grabbed his beer and took a long gulp.

She reached over and touched the scars on his arm. His muscles went rigid and he dragged in a breath. She stroked his forearm, not fazed by the ridges of scar tissue. He hadn't talked about this in such a long time. She didn't say anything, but he could still feel the words bubbling up inside him.

"There was a mission. It was fucked, right from the beginning. Some locals had snitched on us. We came under attack, and three of us were captured by the Taliban. Tortured." Even now, he remembered the screams, the blood, and pain.

Her fingers tangled with his, and air shuddered into his lungs.

"My friends didn't make it."

"I'm so sorry, Diego. You have to know it wasn't your fault. That you did everything you could in a terrible situation."

"I know...but it doesn't make it any easier."

She squeezed his hand. "I lost an agent friend last year. We had intel on a big drug deal going down. We thought the intel was solid and went in, but there were far more cartel members than we'd planned for. Simon went down in a hail of bullets."

There was ragged pain in her voice. He pulled her into his arms and she pressed her face to his chest. They stood there, arms wrapped around each other. Diego felt...something. Something he hadn't felt in a long while. Comfort.

"I know how it feels," she murmured. "I know how much it hurts and how much it haunts you. I keep waiting for time to make it more bearable."

"But you never forget."

"Never." She was quiet a moment. "Your family sounds like they love you."

He sighed. "They do."

"Don't push them away. You never know how long you've got them for. I'm losing my grandfather—" her voice hitched "—and I'd give anything to have more time."

Her words echoed through Diego, and he tightened his hold on her.

Finally, she stepped back, straightening her shoulders. "So, we have a workable salvage plan."

He nodded. "We should get some sleep. We have a lot of diving to do tomorrow."

Her gaze stayed on his, direct and open. "Thanks, Diego. For everything. Good night."

He watched her walk away, his hands balling into fists to stop from reaching for her. He looked down at the scars on his arm, and this time, he wasn't thinking of pain and loss. He was thinking of Sloan's fingers stroking him.

———

SLOAN SLAMMED VIOLENTLY from sleep to wide awake, her chest burning. A heavy weight was pressing down on her face and she couldn't breathe.

She was being smothered with a pillow.

She exploded into action, struggling against her attacker. But the bastard was strong.

Think, Sloan. Think, or you're dead.

She pretended to lose strength, letting her body go

lax. She was gasping for air against the fabric on her face and it wouldn't be long before she wasn't pretending.

Slumping against the bunk, she reached around, her fingers brushing against a bulky, hard thigh encased in a damp wet suit.

From the person's size, it was a man.

She steeled herself, and then punched between his legs. Hard.

A harsh groan echoed through the small cabin. The pressure on the pillow eased, and Sloan thrust herself upward with all her strength.

Then the pillow was gone and she was dragging in air. She leaped off the bunk. It was pitch black in the compact cabin, but she managed to slam into her attacker. She punched him hard—jab, hook, uppercut. Grunts and groans echoed through the small room.

She sent another fist into his belly, and the air exploded out of the man. She moved back enough to land a front kick to his gut.

He staggered into the wall and she punched him again, before following through with a hard elbow to the face.

He went down and was out cold.

Her hand was shaking as she flicked on the light. She went to her duffel bag and grabbed some zip ties. It only took a second to bind him.

She turned his face toward her. Square jaw, ordinary looking, with dark hair. She grabbed her tablet and snapped a picture.

Then she straightened. *Diego*. This thug wouldn't have been alone. Had they gone after Diego, as well?

She snatched up her Glock and slammed out of the cabin. She jogged down the hall. It was illuminated with low lights.

Diego was a SEAL. No way they could have gotten the drop on him.

She threw his cabin door open, but couldn't see a thing. The sliver of light from the hall only illuminated a tiny bit of carpet.

Suddenly, a big body slammed into her, and they hit the floor in a tangle. It was a big, naked body.

"Sloan? What the fuck?" Diego pushed off her.

"I was attacked in my cabin." She sat up. "Silk Road is aboard."

He cursed and reached down to pull her up.

"You okay?" He snapped the light on.

Sloan blinked. "Fine. Idiot tried to smother me." Her tone hardened as she rubbed her chest. "I think he regrets it now."

She saw anger glittering in Diego's dark eyes, then she froze. He was naked. *Very* naked. She already knew he had a hard body with zero body fat. Her gaze skated over his tattoo, and then dropped down.

Focus on the bad guys, inner hussy. But for the first time in her life, she found herself mesmerized by a man's cock. A nice, thick cock.

Diego spun, and she watched as he grabbed some shorts from the cupboard. Her gaze moved over his firm ass and she rolled her eyes to the ceiling. *Down, hussy, down.* Finally, he was covered up, and he pulled his Desert Eagle from the bedside table.

He held the weapon up. "Let's go."

She tightened her grip on her Glock and ignored the fact that she was in her pajama shorts and tank top without a bra.

They crept along the hall, clearing each of the cabins. They moved upstairs, passing through the galley and the labs. Creeping up the stairs to the bridge, they found scratch marks on the door. Silk Road had tried to access the bridge, but Diego's security had kept them out.

Diego motioned back down the stairs. They crept across the deck and when he paused, she spotted the wet footprints. Diego crouched and raised some fingers.

Four intruders. One of which was tied up in her cabin.

Diego stood and continued on, but they hadn't gone far when he cursed under his breath. She followed his gaze.

In the security lights, she saw that the diving equipment had been trashed. Everything was strewn about and cut up. Over by the ROV rack, she saw they hadn't been able to unlock the machines, but she saw shredded lines. They'd still done damage.

No. Her gut clenched.

She watched a muscle tick in Diego's jaw. He waved her on, and they continued their search of the ship.

Finally, he straightened, his shoulders relaxing. "They're no longer aboard."

"What about the guy in my cabin?"

Together, they hurried belowdecks. Her cabin was wrecked from the struggle, the bed covers twisted off the bunk. But the man was gone, clearly rescued by his buddies.

Sloan cursed and kicked the bed.

Diego lowered his gun. "This was a sabotage mission."

"Fucking Silk Road," she bit out.

"They wanted to slow us down and send us back to shore."

"Then they'll sneak in and steal the emerald."

He moved closer, touching her cheek. "We won't let them win. They didn't get into the bridge. They don't have the exact coordinates of the *Atocha*."

She gritted her teeth and nodded. She was so frustrated.

"We'll have to head back to Key West. We need new diving equipment." He stroked her cheek again. "And we need reinforcements. I don't want a repeat of tonight."

"I'm sorry that your equipment was destroyed," she said.

He ran a finger down the slope of her nose. "I don't give a fuck about the equipment, Sloan."

CHAPTER FIVE

A s they sailed back to Key West, Diego fumed.

Once again, Silk Road had boarded his boat under the cover of darkness, attacking innocent people in their sleep. *Cowards*. He'd been pissed the first time it had happened, off the coast of Madagascar on a THS mission, but now he was beyond angry.

He hoped to hell that whatever trap Darcy was planning worked and Silk Road was ground to dust.

Sloan sat quietly beside him on the bridge. Every time he looked at her bloodshot eyes, his anger surged. She could have died. His gut clenched. They'd pay for attacking her.

The hours ticked by, and finally, the lights of Key West appeared on the horizon. Sloan had been quiet for a while, and when he glanced her way, he saw she was asleep.

He realized he'd never seen her look so relaxed. Her

lashes were dark against her skin, and she had a hand tucked under her face. The hunt for the emerald, Silk Road, and losing her grandfather were all taking a toll.

Diego felt a sudden urge to pull her into his lap and protect her from it all. He shook his head. If there was anyone who could take care of herself, it was Sloan McBride.

Finally, he pulled the *Nymph* into the marina. He ducked outside to tie off the boat. When he came back, she was still asleep. He gently touched her shoulder. "Sloan."

She blinked, and when her sleepy gaze fell on him, she smiled. Something in his chest melted.

"We're back already?" she asked.

"Yep. Sun's just rising. I need to contact my equipment guy and find out how long it'll take to get new gear, or get the current stuff repaired."

"I want to get back out there today, Diego."

"I'm not sure how long it'll take. I'll do my best to speed things along."

She stood, shaking off sleep, her face morphing into her DEA agent face—hard and determined. "The quicker we get back out there, the quicker we can stop Silk Road from stealing our emerald."

He smiled. "Our emerald, huh?"

She smiled back. "Yes."

His smile faded. "You need to contact Darcy. We need backup."

Sloan nodded. "I'll call her and see how long it'll take for Treasure Hunter Security to get here."

He nodded. "Snap to it, sailor."

She rolled her eyes and reached for her phone. Diego pulled out his cell and watched her wander out onto the balcony. He made his calls, calling in favors to his main equipment supplier. Bruno could be a pain in the ass, but he had good scuba gear.

Looking out the window, he saw Sloan in deep conversation. He hoped to hell that Dec and his team could get here soon.

There was no way Diego was risking Sloan's life again.

She came back, frowning. "Darcy has to tidy some things up in DC before she can head down. She says Dec's getting the THS team in Mexico to head our way, but it'll take them twenty-four hours to get here." Sloan huffed out a breath. "It's too long."

"We should wait for them."

"We can't, Diego. Silk Road knows the general area we've been diving in. They'll find the Emerald Butterfly."

He blew out a breath. "Okay, but we have to see if we can get the dive equipment first. Come on, let's pay my guy a visit."

DARCY WARD BACKED out of the tight crawlspace beneath the museum exhibit, cursing as she bumped her head.

Sitting back on the polished Travertine tile, she dusted off her hands. "There. Done. The wiring is all set up. Now, I need to get to Florida."

A strong hand gripped her arm and helped her to her feet. "I need you here. This is our chance to take Silk Road down once and for all."

Darcy jerked her arm away and spun. The main exhibit room of the Dashwood Museum was grand and gorgeous. The creamy tile floors contrasted with the glossy wooden walls. Large windows let in loads of sunlight, which helped outline the large frame of Agent Arrogant and Annoying.

As always, Darcy pondered the cosmic joke of how such an unsmiling, irritating, bossy man could look so damn good. A dark suit and tie accented his muscled body. Brown hair was cut short, and as always, he had the shadow of sexy stubble on his hard jaw. He shifted and she caught sight of the handgun holstered at his side.

"Remember, I'm working *with* you, not *for* you, Burke. My friend needs me. Silk Road almost killed her, and this exhibit doesn't open for another week. I'll be back, and we'll be ready by then."

The Dashwood would soon be showing an exhibit of previously unseen artifacts. One of which was shrouded in myth and legend. It was just the kind of artifact that Silk Road liked to acquire, AKA steal, and not care who they hurt and murdered in the process.

"Your brother can go."

"He will, but so will I. Sloan is my friend."

"Sloan McBride is a trained federal agent. How do you think you can help her?"

Darcy stepped forward, her boot heels clicking on the floor. Her toes brushed his shiny black shoes. "Because

I'm smart. I don't need to be a black belt in martial arts or wave a gun around to help my friend."

Burke's intense green eyes flashed. "It could be dangerous."

"Duh, that's why we're going down to help her. That's what friends do." She crossed her arms over her chest. "Don't you have any friends, Burke?"

He scowled at her but didn't answer.

Footsteps. "I have Starbucks."

Another suited agent entered, a smile on his face. He carried a tray of coffees.

Special Agent Thomas Singh looked from Darcy to Burke. "Looks like I'm just in time to stop you two from going a few rounds. Again." He shoved a cup at Darcy. "A vanilla latte, extra shot."

Darcy managed a smile. "You are a god. How the hell do you put up with Agent Scowly all day?"

Burke growled and the sound made Darcy feel pretty darn good. She sipped her latte and moaned. That was good, too.

When she looked up, Burke was staring at her, with a look in his eyes that made her muscles tense. Before she could process it, he swiveled and strode out.

And damn if the man didn't look just as fine from the back as he did from the front. Such a waste.

"So, Thom, I'm headed to Florida for a few days."

"For some sun and sand."

She smiled. "No, for some gunfights and mayhem, probably."

The agent sipped his own drink. "Have fun. See you when you get back."

DIEGO PULLED his Jeep up at the marina parking lot.

Sloan jumped out and slammed the door. "I can't believe we haven't got everything we need!"

"Threatening to arrest Bruno probably wasn't the right move."

Sloan scowled.

Diego gripped her shoulder. "I know you're frustrated. I know you want to be back out there right now, but even if we had all the gear, by the time we got out there, it'd be too late to dive.

"At least we could keep Silk Road away from our site."

"You and me against all of Silk Road. I think I'm flattered."

Her nose wrinkled.

"We're both tired after our fiasco last night, and let's not forget that you almost suffocated." Just saying the words made a muscle tick in his jaw. "Bruno will get the gear here first thing in the morning. Then we'll head back out."

She huffed out a breath. "Fine."

"We won't let Silk Road win."

"Right. Well, I'll put together a late lunch for us." With another frustrated breath, she headed into the galley.

"Thanks."

"Don't thank me yet," she called over her shoulder. "The kitchen is not my area of expertise."

Diego checked the ship and coordinated with the

marina office for refueling. When he finally made it to the galley, a burnt smell assaulted his nose.

An even more frustrated Sloan was slamming around his galley.

"I ruined lunch." She threw her hands in the air.

He struggled to hide his smile. "Well, you are stressed."

She shook her head. "Actually, I burn everything. I'm a terrible cook."

She looked dejected, and he knew it wasn't really about the cooking. "I know you have other skills." He went over to the fridge and pulled out some fresh shrimp, then grabbed a baguette from the cupboard. He grabbed two beers and popped the tops. He handed one to her.

"I do." Sloan leaned against the counter, taking the beer. "I can shoot, I'm an excellent negotiator, and I'm really good at hand-to-hand combat."

"All skills I look for in a woman."

She faced him and raised a brow. "Oh? Don't you want a sweet, lil' thing who'll cook your meals, and stay barefoot and pregnant?"

His gaze dropped to her long legs, heat curling in his gut. "No." He set his beer down. "Don't you want some sharp-jawed, suit-wearing, law-enforcement type?"

She stepped closer to him. "No."

Diego grabbed her, trapping her against the counter. Her hands curled into his shirt, her mouth pressed to his jaw. He gripped her hips and boosted her onto the counter. *Dios*, her mouth. He needed it. He brought her lips to his and drank deep. The kiss had a hard, needy edge.

Her hands twisted in his T-shirt, then she tore it up over his head.

"I need you, Diego. I need hot, rough, and hard."

He groaned. "Hell, yeah."

He worked the buttons of her shirt loose and cupped her breasts through her bra. She leaned forward and bit his bottom lip, her legs clamping onto his hips.

Diego dropped his hands, tearing her shorts open. Then he ripped them and her panties off. He slid his hands between her thighs, stroking her. She moaned.

"You like that?" His voice was guttural. "You're so wet for me, *chiquita.*"

"Yes." Her hips undulated against his hand. "God, Diego."

"I want you to come like this, on my fingers." He pumped two inside her.

"Yes. Oh, like that."

Diego felt her body tighten, her moans increasing. A second later, her thighs clenched, and she came with a cry. Watching her pleasure wash over her had vicious need clamping down on him.

He pulled her right to the edge of the counter. Her hands went to his shorts, fumbling with the zipper. He grabbed his wallet and yanked out a foil packet. His cock sprang free.

"Need to fuck you," he growled, opening the condom and sliding it on.

"Do it," she panted.

He notched the head of his cock against her warm folds, and a second later, he slammed inside her. "Finally."

"Yes," Sloan moaned.

Damn, she was tight, clasping him hard. She felt like heaven. "I've wanted you for months."

Her lips parted, her gaze on his face. "Me, too."

"Sloan—"

She wiggled against him. "Move, Torres."

Still busting his balls. *Dios*, she was perfect. Diego did as ordered.

GOD, they fit. Perfectly.

Sloan held on tight as Diego powered inside her. She pressed her mouth to his throat, tasting his salty skin. He felt so good, so thick and hard. He filled her up.

She shifted her legs, gripping his sides. She pushed her hips up to meet his thrusts.

"Diego."

"I love hearing you say my name like that, *chiquita*. Especially when I'm buried inside you."

His mouth took hers and they strained against each other.

"Give it to me, Sloan. Let me hear you come."

"God." She writhed on the cool surface of the counter. Sensations poured through her and she slid her hands into his hair. She tugged hard and she knew he'd feel it.

Her orgasm hit her and she jerked, crying out his name.

Then he pulled out of her, his cock still rock-hard and glistening. She cried out in protest.

Before she could say anything, he scooped her up off the counter like she weighed nothing, and strode out of the galley.

"The next time, we come together," he growled.

As he stepped out onto the deck, she didn't even care that they were naked. He quickly carried her belowdecks, and before she knew it, they entered his shadowed cabin.

He dropped her on the bed and, before she moved, he gripped her and flipped her over.

"Diego." Her voice was husky with excitement.

"On your knees." He gripped her hips.

She rose and felt his big body behind her. Her heart pounded. She'd never had such intense, out-of-control sex before. She loved it.

One of his hands gripped her hair, pulling her head back. His mouth took hers, tongue sliding against hers.

And then his cock pushed inside her again. She moaned.

His other hand moved, cupping her hip, and then his body was moving. God, he was fucking her hard. His skin smacked against her ass.

"You feel so good, Sloan. So tight around my cock."

Then his hand slid beneath her and stroked her swollen clit. No, she couldn't possibly come again....

"Diego." A strangled cry.

Sloan tipped over the edge, crying out his name again. Then Diego lodged deep inside her, stiffened, and growled as he came.

He collapsed forward, but shifted so they lay on their sides. He pulled her close, their sweaty skin sticking them together.

Sloan was just trying to breathe again. Diego's lips touched her shoulder, and she shivered.

"We fit," he murmured.

CHAPTER SIX

S loan woke to lips moving down her body.

She smiled in the morning sunshine, sliding her hand into Diego's hair. *Wowser*. She'd just had the best night of her life. She'd never had that many orgasms all in a row, and she now knew that Diego had impressive stamina and was all kinds of creative.

She looked down at him and damn, he looked so sexy with all that sleek, brown skin and those slumberous eyes.

"Morning," she murmured.

"Morning, *chiquita*." He nipped at her belly and moved lower.

Oh, God. She pressed her head into the pillows, feeling the stroke of his fingers on her inner thigh. She knew what was coming next and she shivered. The man was very good with his mouth.

Then suddenly, he stiffened.

Sloan blinked, and that's when she heard it...footsteps on the deck above.

Diego leaped up, moving quickly. He yanked on his denim shorts and grabbed his gun. Then he was gone.

"Wait." Sloan jumped out of the bed. Where were her clothes? *Dammit.* They were strewn across the galley upstairs.

She needed to have Diego's back. SEAL or no SEAL, she wasn't leaving him to face whoever the hell was up there alone.

She ripped the sheet off the bed and wrapped it around her body. Then she rummaged through Diego's drawer, from where he'd grabbed his handgun, and found a nice SIG Sauer. She snatched it up, checked it, and loaded it. She raced out of the cabin and headed up on deck.

Blinking against the bright sunshine, she frowned, her steps slowing. She could hear Diego speaking in Spanish. He spoke so fast she couldn't keep up, but he sounded pissed.

SIG held up, she slowly rounded the wall and jerked to a halt.

A small, round, dark-haired woman in her sixties stood on the deck, facing off with Diego. Beside her was a curvy, younger version of the woman, with a glorious sheet of dark hair.

Diego stood there, his bare back to Sloan, and his handgun held by his side.

The women noticed Sloan at the same moment, and dark eyes widened.

Shit. It took Sloan two seconds to see that the younger woman was a female version of Diego, and had to be his sister. Sloan lowered the SIG, fighting back a blush.

"*Ay Dios mio*," the older woman breathed, her eyes glittering.

Diego looked back over his shoulder. The anger drained out of him, and his lips twitched.

"Ah, hello," Sloan said.

"Hello, I'm Maria." The older woman bustled forward. "I'm Diego's mama, and this is his sister, Teresa."

The younger woman had a huge smile on her face. She waggled her fingers at Sloan.

"Nice to meet you both." *While I'm dressed in a sheet, holding a gun, and having just spent the night doing naughty, dirty things with your son.* "I'm Sloan. Sloan McBride."

"And you're single, Sloan?" Mrs. Torres said. "Do you work? Go to church?"

"Ah—" The rapid-fire questions made Sloan look at Diego, trying to tell him with her eyes to help her.

But he was smiling down at the deck, his hands on his hips.

Bastard. "I'm an agent with the DEA."

Maria Torres' eyes went wide. "Oh. Well, a government job is good. Good benefits and stability."

"And Diego needs a badass woman, Mama," Teresa said.

Oh, God. "Diego is helping me with a job. Some diving and salvage." She looked at him again, rolling her eyes. *Help me.*

"Mama, we need to get to work," Diego said. "Here's

Bruno now with the dive equipment we've been waiting for."

Sloan turned her head and spotted the bald-headed Bruno, and another man, hauling tanks across the dock walkways.

She cleared her throat. "Well, it was nice to meet you."

More Spanish spilled out of Mrs. Torres. She gestured at Diego.

He let out a breath. "Okay, okay, Ma. Now go."

"Bye, Sloan." Mrs. Torres' smile was wide. She grabbed Teresa's arm, and the two women waved as they headed down the ramp.

"What did she say?" Sloan hissed.

"We've been invited to dinner after we finish our job."

"What?" she breathed.

Diego wrapped an arm around her shoulder and pressed a kiss to the top of her head. "My mama is planning to cook her world-famous chicken tostadas."

"What?" Sloan said again. It was all she could manage. "I can't have dinner with your family."

He looked down at her. "You're not going to disappoint my mama, are you?"

Sloan narrowed her gaze. "Are you trying to blackmail me?"

"Maybe. What are you going to do? Cuff me?" He nipped her lips. "I'm sorry we got interrupted earlier."

She melted. "Me, too."

"Want to get dressed before Bruno comes aboard?"

Eek. "Yes." She wasn't facing anyone else in a sheet. She darted off down belowdecks.

After a quick shower, Sloan pulled on fresh clothes. She was heading up to the deck when she felt the ship's engines rumble to life. She found Diego on the bridge, pulling them out of the marina.

"We have everything?" she asked.

He nodded. "Ready to roll."

As they hit the open ocean, he increased the speed. Sloan's nerves were clanging. What if Silk Road had found the emerald? What if they were out there now, and they were forced into a confrontation? She chewed on the end of her nail. Maybe they should've waited for Dec, Darcy, and the others to arrive.

"Stay calm," Diego said.

"I can't."

"What do you do when you're waiting to make a bust? You must do something to stay in control?"

She felt heat in her cheeks. "I...uh, recite the lyrics to Broadway tunes in my head."

He smiled. "You like musicals."

"Yes. So? Lots of people do."

"I always stopped and took a second to breathe in the smells. Cooking, vegetation, perfume. It helped to block out all the extraneous stuff and let me focus."

Sloan breathed deep. "I smell you." Musky male and the sea. And damned if her edginess didn't ease a little.

"And I smell your delicious and distracting shampoo."

"Distracting, huh?"

"Ever since I first laid eyes on you."

She smiled at him. Her edginess didn't disappear, but she felt more focused. She stood beside him, watching out the window as they neared the site.

"We've arrived," he said.

Sloan leaned forward. There were no signs of any other boats in the area. Her shoulders relaxed.

Diego cut the engines. "Ready to dive?"

"Let's do it."

They fell into the routine they'd formed the other day. They helped each other into their dive gear, and soon were back in the water. They descended and moved back to the area where they'd found the small emerald.

Diego directed her into a search grid. As she swam, she tried to imagine what the captain's cabin had looked like in its heyday. A grizzled man sitting behind a wooden desk, with his cabin boy bustling in and out. It was hard to believe that so little was left now—just rotted and encrusted ruins resting below the sea.

She spotted the gleam of something in the sand and hurried over. She pried up some rocks, and her heart gave a thump. She held up a chunky, gold cross on a thick chain.

It was stunning and she knew it would be worth a fortune. But it wasn't the Emerald Butterfly.

Had it rested with the lost Incan artifact? Had they been locked together in the captain's cabin?

Diego appeared, shaking out a small mesh bag. He held it out and she gently eased the necklace into it. He clipped it to her belt.

They kept searching, and next, Diego found a gold chalice. It gleamed dully in the water.

But no emerald.

Sloan lifted her head, scanning the azure water around them. *Where are you?*

"JUST ONE MORE DIVE," Sloan pleaded, already pulling her wet suit on.

They'd pulled up several gold artifacts from the wreck, and all of the pieces were now safely stored in the wet lab. Diego looked to the western horizon. It was still a few hours until sunset, but they were already losing the light.

"We'll lose the light while we're down there," he said.

She shimmied her hips to get the wet suit on, and his gaze dropped to her body.

"We'll make it a quick dive." She winked. "And I promise you some naked sexual favors later."

He cocked his head. "Agent McBride, are you bribing me?"

"Yep." She grinned.

"Deal. But I get to pick which favors." *Dios*, he was easy when it came to this woman. Being with Sloan was good. Beyond good. They worked well together, had smoking chemistry, and she made him smile.

Shaking his head, he pulled his gear on, and helped Sloan slide into her fresh tanks. After a quick kiss, they tumbled into the water.

They headed back to the search grid, and he was right, it wasn't long before he could tell visibility was dropping.

They found a few more artifacts—mostly ceramic pieces. Diego held up an old clay smoking pipe and wondered if it had belonged to the *Atocha's* captain. Had he puffed on this, contemplating where his ship would take them? Little had he known that a hurricane would send his ship and her treasure to the bottom of the sea.

Diego checked his dive watch. They didn't have much longer before they needed to head back to the *Nymph*.

He watched Sloan digging carefully through the sand. Just beyond her, he saw movement in the murk, and stiffened. The sleek shadow of a shark sliced through the water. A reef shark, thankfully. It was bull sharks he hated running into the most. But as he spotted the reef shark darting closer, he saw this one was curious, and it was big.

And probably hungry.

With a flick of his fins, Diego moved closer to Sloan and pulled his spear gun off his belt. The shark swam closer, and Diego nudged Sloan. He held his palm upright in front of his face in the sign for shark.

She watched it and nodded. Just as she turned back to her search, the shark darted in close again, and bumped her.

She spun around, and Diego raised his spear gun. The animal was coming in aggressively.

Sloan didn't panic or flail. No, she just moved back a little and stayed cool. Her fins did hit the sand, sending up a cloud.

The shark shot forward, and Diego fired the spear

gun. Quickly, the reef shark reversed course and disappeared into the gloom.

Diego grabbed Sloan's arm. *Okay?*

She held her hand up to signal back. *Okay.*

Then, she looked down, and started waving her arms.

At first, he was worried that the shark had hurt her, but then he saw her pointing. He looked down at the sand.

Her fins had dug a shallow hole, and resting in the center of it was a huge emerald.

Jesus, it was big. The Emerald Butterfly.

He waved at her, and she lowered down to the emerald. She lifted it reverently and held it in front of her. Through her mask, Diego could tell that she was moved by the moment.

This wasn't just about treasure for Sloan.

Carefully, he held the mesh bag open, and she set the gem inside. They wasted no time ascending and climbing back aboard the *Storm Nymph.*

"Oh, God. Oh, God." Sloan did a quick dance, pulling Diego close and smacking a kiss on his lips. She pulled the emerald out, holding it up. It was large and irregularly shaped. He could see the vague shape of the butterfly that had given it its name.

"Granddad won't believe it!" She hugged the jewel to her chest. "It's been his dream all his life to find this."

Diego wrapped an arm around her shoulders and hugged her. He turned her toward the setting sun. The entire horizon was painted a brilliant gold that bled out into an amazing orange. As they stood there, he realized he liked her here. On his deck, burning his lunch, sleeping in his bed.

Shit. He'd never wanted to keep a woman before. But Sloan—smart, tough, sexy Sloan who loved her grandfather—was one-of-a-kind.

She had Diego caught, and this was one net that he didn't want to get out of.

Suddenly, something out on the water caught his eye. He jerked his head up.

Sloan stiffened. "What is it?"

He saw the outlines of the inflatable boats racing toward them.

"Fuck." He grabbed Sloan's hand and pulled her toward the bridge. They took the stairs two at a time.

Inside, he yanked out his binoculars. He held them up and got a closer look. Five boats, each one filled with four men. He handed the binoculars to Sloan.

She looked, her face turning hard. "Silk Road."

With a nod, he turned and started the engines. He quickly turned the *Storm Nymph,* and built up her speed.

Sloan rested her hands on the console. "They're faster than us."

He nodded. "At least twice our top speed, maybe more."

Her hands curled. "Then I guess there'll be a firefight."

Dios, this woman. "Weapons locker is over there." He pointed to the far wall. "I'll tell you the code."

He shouted out the numbers, and watched as she opened the locker and studied his collection.

Diego touched his console and quickly tapped in a

message to Declan. It looked like Treasure Hunter Security would be too late to help this time.

Sloan pulled out a rifle, checking it over.

"The emerald?" he asked.

She patted her pocket. "Zipped up safely." She looked at him, her face set. "Let's do this."

CHAPTER SEVEN

D iego heard Sloan firing on the incoming boats. He flicked on the external cameras, and watched the inflatable boats chasing after them. They were gaining.

Sloan fired again, and he saw one of the boats flip. Men tumbled into the water.

Four boats were still incoming.

Steps echoed outside and Sloan reappeared. "They're almost on us."

He nodded and stopped the *Nymph*. They slowed down and came to a stop. He watched her at the weapons locker, swapping out the rifle for two handguns. She shoved extra ammunition into her pockets.

"Plan?" she asked.

Diego grabbed his own weapons out of the locker. "Take out as many as we can, and then hijack a boat."

She sucked in a shocked breath. "And leave the *Nymph*?"

It hurt. The thought of abandoning his baby hurt a lot.

But he had to get Sloan to safety, and that was more important.

"They don't want the *Nymph*. I'll come back for her."

Sloan nodded and together they ducked out of the bridge. Darkness was falling as he led her out onto the deck and to a small alcove set into one of the equipment racks. They stopped there, hiding in the shadows.

It wasn't long before they heard the whine of the engines on the inflatable boats. The sound cut off. Then Diego heard quiet, furtive movements across the deck.

Silk Road was aboard.

He nodded at Sloan, and a moment later, two figures slunk into view, completely unaware that Diego and Sloan were hiding there.

Diego held up a hand, waiting, waiting. Then he lunged forward and slammed into the first shadow. Out of the corner of his eye, he saw Sloan go in low, kicking the second man's knees out from under him.

They kept it quiet, subduing the men. Sloan shoved her attacker facedown onto the deck, and seconds later, she pulled out a roll of duct tape and zip ties. Diego shook his head, fighting a grin. *Dios*, she was something.

After binding the men's ankles and wrists, and covering their mouths with tape, Diego dragged them both in behind some equipment where they wouldn't be found.

Then he heard footsteps on the deck, and people heading down to the cabins below.

"Find them," someone called out.

Diego motioned to Sloan, and they slipped into the shadows. She moved well and kept up with him, keeping her movements quiet.

They neared the railings on the starboard side of the ship, and Diego quickly ducked his head over. He saw the four inflatables tied up below, with no one aboard them. He nodded at her. There was a rope leading up to the railing, and he pointed at it, motioning for her to climb down.

She tucked her gun in the back of her shorts and climbed over the railing. She'd just grabbed on the rope and started down, when a big man appeared. "Hey!"

Diego rammed into the man. "Keep going."

As he and the man wrestled, he saw Sloan shimmy out of view. Straining against the Silk Road thug, he gritted his teeth. Damn, he was a big sucker. Diego rammed a fist into the man's gut, then grabbed him again as they slammed into the railing. It was a vicious struggle, and Diego took an elbow to the chest, which knocked the air out of him.

Grimacing, he held on. He shoved the guy and managed a punch to his jaw. A second later, he landed an uppercut to the man's gut, and sent the thug staggering back against the railing.

Diego spun, ducking behind the man, and got an arm around his neck. Diego pulled back, putting all his weight into it, exerting pressure on the man's windpipe.

The man struggled hard, but he was rapidly losing consciousness. Diego grimly held on, ignoring the aches from the hits the man had gotten in. Then the thug slumped over.

Diego dropped him and heard shouts nearby. *Shit*.

He looked over the railing and saw Sloan in one of the inflatables. She started the engine, waving at him. There was no time for him to climb down. Diego climbed up on the railing, took a breath, and leaped.

He landed in the boat and sent it rocking wildly. Sloan spun and coolly aimed her Glock up at the *Nymph*. She fired a few shots, and above, Diego heard shouts and swearing.

Then she turned and fired at the two closest inflatables. Bullets pinged off their engines. His smart woman was trying to sabotage them.

He quickly grabbed the tiller on their engine. "Hold on."

She gripped a built-in handle, and he punched the accelerator. They sped away from the ship.

Diego glanced back, ignoring the sharp pang in his chest. He was abandoning his ship, but keeping Sloan safe. He watched several Silk Road men leaping into the other inflatables. Two of the boats tore away in pursuit.

Gunfire lit up the night. "Keep holding on!"

Sloan nodded, crouching down. He started swerving the boat, taking evasive maneuvers. Then she raised her gun and returned fire.

"Stay down!" he yelled.

She waved a hand at him. Suddenly, their engine coughed, and their speed reduced. *Fuck*. Their engine had been hit. It was still functioning, but it had been damaged.

The Silk Road boats were gaining on them. Spotlights from the boats cut through the night. Diego kept swerving and soon, he was weaving in and out of the other two boats, trying to stop him and Sloan being peppered with bullets.

One of the boats pulled up close beside them. Diego raised his gun and fired.

All of a sudden, a man leaped off and landed on their boat. *Shit.* The thug was half in half out of the boat, gripping the side.

Sloan reached him, and hammered his hand with the butt of her pistol. He roared at her, but she bent down, got her weight under him, and heaved.

The man fell overboard with a shout.

"You are one hell of a woman, Sloan McBride," Diego yelled.

She grinned at him, but another barrage of gunfire had her ducking down.

Suddenly, Diego felt a burning pain on his left arm. The impact spun him away from the controls.

"Diego! You're hit."

He pushed back the pain, blinking through it. He looked into Sloan's white face, and knew he was bleeding. *Dammit.* He slapped a hand over his seeping bicep.

SLOAN YANKED HER SHIRT OFF, leaving her in just her bikini top. She pressed it to Diego's shoulder, trying to control her churning stomach. Thankfully, the adrenaline pumping through her was helping her cope.

"Those bastards shot you," she said between gritted teeth.

Silk Road had to be stopped, once and for all.

"Winged me. It's fine."

"It's bleeding everywhere." Which she was trying to ignore. For a second, she remembered Simon dying in that horrible, drug-riddled warehouse. "They shot you. Fucking Silk Road." She *wasn't* losing Diego.

Anger geysered up inside her like an eruption.

Diego's lips quirked. "I've been shot before, Sloan. This just clipped me."

"I don't care. I'm going to arrest *every single one* of them for shooting my man."

He gripped the controls and the boat swerved. One of the Silk Road boats shot past them.

Diego looked at her. "Your man?"

She tossed her head back. "Yes. Got a problem with that?"

He smiled. "No. No, I don't."

She gave him a nod, and quickly tied her shirt around his arm. Then she turned, raised her weapon, and took several shots at the closest boat.

It was then that their engine spluttered.

Diego's smile dissolved. "Dammit, it's about to die completely!"

Sloan scanned around, but she could see nothing but dark, open ocean. There was no help.

She felt the heavy weight of the Emerald Butterfly in her pocket. Silk Road would take it, kill her and Diego, and her granddad would die alone.

The engine died, and their boat drifted to a stop.

Grimly, Sloan reloaded her pistols. "They are *not* killing us."

Diego lifted his own weapon and pulled her close.

Without the roar of the engine, she now heard the steady *thwap thwap* of helicopter rotors. She swiveled and saw the lights of an incoming chopper in the sky. Her stomach dropped. Damn, they were completely outgunned and outnumbered.

The two boats zoomed toward them, circling around. Diego yanked her in for a quick kiss.

"Ready to fight?" he asked.

She breathed in his now-familiar sea scent. "I'm ready."

As the lead boat drifted closer, she spotted one Silk Road thug grinning at them nastily. The helicopter was almost on them, its bright light shining down.

Sloan set her shoulders back. Whatever happened, she'd fight. And she'd do it with Diego by her side. She wasn't alone.

Bam.

The thug jerked, a spray of blood misting into the air. He tipped over, into the water.

Sloan froze. *What the hell?*

She looked up and saw Declan Ward hanging out the side of the chopper with a rifle in his hand.

Dec looked down his scope and kept firing. Two figures leaped out of the helicopter, lowering down on ropes. In the chopper's lights, she could see a tall, dark-haired woman and a big man with shaggy hair firing as they rappelled down.

Diego elbowed her and Sloan turned. Together, they lifted their weapons, firing at the boat closest to them. Soon, there was no one left standing in the boat.

The other boat turned, trying to escape. It zoomed away, but a small object dropped from the chopper and splashed into the water.

A second later, the grenade exploded right beside the Silk Road boat. The giant spray of water lifted the inflatable into the air and flipped it over.

Dec saluted Sloan and Diego, as the helicopter flew over them to circle around. She saw Cal Ward at the controls, and Darcy waving madly from the co-pilot seat.

Diego wrapped an arm around Sloan and she leaned into him and laughed. "I still owe you some sexual favors, Torres."

He squeezed her. "Yes, you do, Agent McBride. I won't forget."

Then he kissed her. It was a kiss brimming with emotion, excitement, adrenaline, and the thrill of surviving. But Sloan felt other things churning inside her. Things she was afraid to name.

Then she saw the blood on his arm and covered her eyes. "Maybe we should stop that bleeding first." The adrenaline of the chase was waning and all she could see now was his bright-red blood.

"My poor, squeamish, Sloan." His lips touched her temple. "Your secret is safe with me, *chiquita*, as long as you promise to nurse me back to health."

She snorted. "It only *winged* you, Torres."

CHAPTER EIGHT

Sloan stood by the railing of the *Storm Nymph* as Diego pulled it smoothly into its berth in the marina. The sun had just risen, and the cool, morning breeze ruffled her hair.

She saw the flashing red-and-blue lights waiting on the docks. A crowd had gathered down on the floating walkway.

"There's the cavalry."

Darcy's words held a sarcastic edge. Sloan's friend stood there, looking as chic as ever in her tight, dark jeans, and a dark-blue shirt. Her dark hair was in a tidy, sleek bob around her face.

After they'd taken out the Silk Road inflatables, they'd retaken the *Storm Nymph*. Sloan had made a mental note to never piss off the THS team. Declan's team were badasses, especially his female security specialist, Morgan. Sloan was pretty sure she had a girl crush on the woman.

The helicopter was now parked on the landing pad at the front of the *Nymph*, and down on the main deck, a dozen Silk Road people were kneeling, hands and feet zip-tied, under the guard of a cranky-looking Logan O'Connor.

Sloan glanced up at the bridge and could see Diego through the window. He stood at the helm, a white bandage on his arm. The THS guys were all decent medics, and the handsome Hale Carter had patched him up.

Diego spotted her looking and his lips quirked. He shot her a quick wink.

"Oh, jeez, not you, too," Darcy muttered.

"What?" Sloan said.

Darcy rolled her blue-gray eyes. "You're falling in love."

Was she? Sloan's heart knocked against her ribs. Oh God, she was.

Darcy smiled. "I can't fault your taste, though. Diego is a good man, and *sooo* easy on the eyes."

Sloan frowned. "Hey, find your own man to ogle."

A flash of something crossed Darcy's face, and then she waved an airy hand in front of her. "The good ones are all taken."

Panic locked Sloan's chest. "What if it doesn't work out?" She swallowed. "Darce, everyone I love leaves me."

"Hey." Darcy wrapped an arm around her. "Losing your family and your grandfather being sick has nothing to do with you, that's just shitty luck, Sloan. I've never met a more courageous, determined woman. You deserve happiness and you sure as hell deserve a good man who loves you. And never forget that I love you."

Sloan hugged her back. "Love you too, babe."

"There are no guarantees in relationships, but I grew up with my totally-in-love parents and watched both my brothers take the fall, not to mention lots of our friends." Darcy's voice softened. "From what I can tell, it's totally worth the risk."

Sloan's gaze drifted up to Diego again. He was in profile and just looking at him made her smile. Yeah, so worth the risk.

Darcy waggled her fingers. "Now, let me see the emerald."

Fishing it out, Sloan held it up. The early morning sunlight hit it, reflecting green fire.

"Gorgeous," Darcy breathed.

"I can't wait to show granddad."

Darcy squeezed Sloan's arm. "I'm here for you, Sloan, whatever you need." Then Darcy glanced up at Diego. "And I think you've got someone else looking out for you now, too."

Sloan wasn't sure what Diego wanted. He'd been hiding from his family and deeper connections for two years now. Was he ready for more? Did he want her to stick around? Did he feel the same shiny mass of emotions inside him that she did?

The *Nymph's* engines cut off, and a second later, FBI agents swarmed onto the deck.

A dark-haired man strode in the lead. Dark suit, dark shades, and a serious face.

Now, Sloan worked with men in suits and holsters every day, but even she had to admit this man was sexy as hell. He fell well out of the neat-and-handsome category, and right into rugged-and-don't-mess-with-me. This was a man who knew how to handle himself.

Darcy groaned.

Sloan raised a brow, noting that the FBI agent was clearly focused on Darcy. He stopped when he reached them.

"Agent McBride, I'm Special Agent Alastair Burke, with the FBI's Art Crime Team."

This was the agent Darcy was working with? "A pleasure." She watched about ten different emotions slide across Darcy's face. *Very interesting.*

"You've had a busy few days," Burke said.

Sloan smiled. "Oh, a few bullets, a boat chase, attempted murder, and a million-dollar Incan emerald. Not that busy. The day's still young."

There was the faintest flicker of a smile on Burke's face before his gaze settled back on Darcy. "I need you back in DC."

Darcy tapped her boot on the deck. "Ask, Burke. Nicely. Real people use their manners."

"I have a plane waiting at Miami International."

"Burke—"

"I'll give you a ride." He swiveled and strode off, issuing orders at the agents processing the Silk Road people.

Darcy let out a half growl, half scream. "That man."

"Speaking of easy on the eyes..."

Darcy held up a hand. "No. He's so damn arrogant."

Sloan shook her head. "Just sleep with him already, and get it over with."

"What?" Darcy's eyes bugged out of her head.

"The sexual tension between the two of you is scorching. I feel like I need a cigarette, or to drag Diego down to his cabin again."

Darcy groaned. "Do not rub your orgasms in my face." She skewered Agent Burke's back with a dark look. "And there is *no* sexual tension. It's just regular, I-hate-his-guts tension."

As though he felt her gaze, Burke turned and looked back. Even with his glasses on, Sloan felt scorched.

She crossed her arms. "Really?"

"Yes, really." Darcy threw her arms around Sloan and hugged her. "I have to go."

"You're avoiding the subject."

"You bet. Take care of yourself, and your emerald." Darcy winked. "And your hunky ex-SEAL."

Sloan hugged her back. "Thanks, Darce. For everything."

DARCY SAT BACK in the plush leather seat of the private jet and focused on reading the file in her hand. The steady drone of the plane engines should have soothed her, but she was still feeling edgy.

One, from rescuing Sloan and Diego from Silk Road, and two, from bantering with Agent Arrogant and

Annoying all the way to the airport. The man was *so* highhanded and bossy.

She dragged in a breath. She was so glad that Sloan and Diego were okay. It had been so damn close. Even now, she remembered sitting in the chopper, watching those speeding boats and gunfire.

Her hands clenched on the file. It was time for Silk Road to pay for all the lives they'd harmed and all the artifacts they'd stolen.

She felt Burke staring at her, his gaze like a laser beam. She lowered the file. "What?"

Green eyes cut into her. "Nothing."

He'd taken off his jacket when they'd boarded. He wore a crisp white shirt with his holster. No wrinkles for Agent Alastair Burke. His handgun was snug under his arm.

Darcy cleared her throat. "So, we still have some work to finish on the exhibit."

He nodded. "We'll get it done before it opens."

"You think the plan will work?"

"Yes."

So certain and sure. She'd never seen Burke flustered or undecided. She hated to admit it, but she admired his confidence. Except when it crossed over into arrogance, which was a lot. Not for the first time, she wondered what drove Burke, what fueled his dedication to his job.

"You really think the Collector will come to DC?" she continued. "You really think we can end Silk Road once and for all?" She wanted it more than anything. The group had attacked her brothers and friends more times than she could count.

Burke leaned forward, his legs brushing hers. She caught a whiff of his yummy cologne—citrus and spice.

"I do. The Collector will come because you and I are baiting the perfect trap for him. And we'll take him and his ring of thieves down because I always get my man." Burke's gaze slid over her face. "Or woman."

Heat ignited in Darcy's belly. Spending so much time with Burke was making it really, really hard for her to live in Darcy Deluded World, where she could deny just how attracted she was to him.

This man confused her. He challenged her, annoyed her, and made her feel alive and out of control. It scared the bejesus out of her.

He rose and Darcy quickly pushed to her feet. Her heart was beating hard and fast. "Burke—"

Suddenly, there was a muffled *thump* and the plane lurched, starting a hard descent.

Darcy was thrown off balance and slammed into Burke's hard chest. One strong arm wrapped around her. He dropped into a seat, holding her tight.

"Anderson," Burke barked.

"Sorry, sir," the pilot called back, voice strained.

The plane engines whined, and Darcy looked out the window and gasped. She could see *smoke*. She gripped onto Burke's shirt.

"Looks like sabotage," Anderson yelled back. "There was some kind of explosion in the engine."

Oh, God. Oh, God. Darcy's heart was thumping so hard it felt like it was going to burst out of her chest. This was Silk Road. It had to be.

Burke thrust her into the seat beside his and did her belt up.

"Alastair—"

His head whipped up and he cupped her cheek. "Not going to let anything happen to you, Darcy."

She stared into his green eyes, absorbing his strength and certainty, and prayed that was true.

"THANKS, DEC."

Declan Ward smiled and shook Diego's hand. "Anytime. You know that."

Diego nodded. "If you hadn't arrived when you did..."

"Hey, it all worked out. At THS we specialize at arriving in the nick of time."

Diego's gaze moved to where Sloan was laughing with Morgan, Logan, and Hale. She was alive and the sound of her laughter worked through him.

"You're fine." Dec clapped a hand on Diego's shoulder. "And the oh-so-sexy and take-charge Sloan is fine as well."

Turning his head, Diego scowled at his friend. "No need for you to notice she's sexy."

Dec barked out a laugh. "I have twenty-twenty vision, buddy. But don't get your cutoffs in a twist, I'm a happily married man, remember? She's gorgeous, smart, and from the looks of things, totally into you. You're a lucky bastard."

ERROR

 177

Diego saw Sloan was looking his way, a smile on her lips. "She's…" He couldn't put everything he was feeling into words.

In the middle of this dangerous treasure hunt, they hadn't had a chance to talk about what had happened between them. Or what the future might hold.

He got a hard slap on the back from Dec. "I know exactly how you feel, Diego. Feel it every time I look at Layne. Speaking of which, I'm going to take my team and head for our jet. I'm feeling very eager to see my wife."

"You aren't going back to DC?"

"Darcy has it under control. I'll be back when the exhibition opens."

"You really think you can catch the Collector and bring down Silk Road."

Dec's eyes hardened. "Hell, yeah. Gonna take his ass down." Dec clasped Diego's hand and they shook. "See you soon."

"Thanks again, Dec."

Diego saw that Sloan was now on her phone and headed for the bridge. Finally, his ship was empty of people.

He tapped on the console. There were no bad guys and no FBI agents. Sloan appeared, her arms wrapped around her middle.

"You spoke with your grandfather," he said.

She nodded. "He's so excited about the emerald." Her smile slipped. "He sounded tired though. I need to book a flight to Denver to see him and show him the Butterfly."

Every muscle in Diego's body locked tight. The thought of her leaving him...

Sloan tucked a strand of hair behind her ear, watching him. "You can get back to your vacation, now."

Diego stalked toward her.

She didn't move but licked her lips. "I guess I'll head back to my job, soon, too."

He grabbed her. "You are not leaving."

She raised a brow. "I'm not?"

"You owe me sexual favors."

"Is that all you want from me?"

"No." He kissed her, hard, like he could communicate everything he was feeling through that kiss. He pulled back, both of them panting. "I want everything, Sloan. I want to see your clothes in my cabin and mine at your place. I want to watch my mama fuss over feeding you. I want to come to Denver with you and meet your grandfather."

Her face softened. "Really?"

"Really. I want your body and—" he took a deep breath "—I'm pretty sure I want your heart, as well."

"Diego." She went up on her toes, resting her forehead against his. "I want that, too."

He lowered his voice. "I'd really like you to bring your handcuffs home sometimes, too."

She flashed him a smile. "What would your mother say?"

"I'm not planning to let her know, but as long as you make me happy, and there's the possibility you might give her grandbabies one day, she won't care." Sloan's laughter warmed his chest. "I want to be your family, *chiquita*, and

I'd like to share mine with you. I haven't been treating them very well, so I've got a lot to make up for."

There was a gleam in her eyes. "I think I can help you with that. Now, stop talking and kiss me, Torres."

He yanked her closer. "It'll be my pleasure, Agent McBride. Now, about those sexual favors..."

———

I hope you enjoyed Oliver and Persephone's story and seeing how the Wards first met, and Diego and Sloan's story too!

Treasure Hunter Security concludes with UNDETECTED, starring Darcy Ward and Agent Arrogant and Annoying, Alastair Burke. You won't want to miss out on their action-packed story, so preorder *Undetected* now.

And stay tuned for more action-packed adventures with the launch of my brand new series, TEAM 52. This features the mysterious team in black the Treasure Hunter Security gang has encountered on their expeditions. Coming in August 2018.

For more action romance, read on for a preview of the first chapter of *Among Galactic Ruins,* the first book in my award-winning Phoenix Adventures series. This is action, adventure, romance, and treasure hunting in space!

Don't miss out! For updates about new releases, action romance info, free books, and other fun stuff, sign up for my VIP mailing list and get your *free box set* containing three action-packed romances.

Visit here to get started: www.annahackettbooks.com

FREE BOX SET DOWNLOAD

JOIN THE ACTION-PACKED ADVENTURE!

MORE ACTION ROMANCE?

**ACTION
ADVENTURE
TREASURE HUNTS
SEXY SCI-FI ROMANCE**

When astro-archeologist and museum curator Dr. Lexa Carter discovers a secret map to a lost old Earth treasure—a priceless Fabergé egg—she's excited at the prospect of a treasure hunt to the dangerous desert planet of Zerzura. What she's not so happy about is being saddled with a bodyguard—the museum's mysterious new head of security, Damon Malik.

After many dangerous years as a galactic spy, Damon

Malik just wanted a quiet job where no one tried to kill him. Instead of easy work in a museum full of artifacts, he finds himself on a backwater planet babysitting the most infuriating woman he's ever met.

She thinks he's arrogant. He thinks she's a trouble-magnet. But among the desert sands and ruins, adventure led by a young, brash treasure hunter named Dathan Phoenix, takes a deadly turn. As it becomes clear that someone doesn't want them to find the treasure, Lexa and Damon will have to trust each other just to survive.

As the descending starship hit turbulence, Dr. Alexa Carter gasped, her stomach jumping.

But she didn't feel sick, she felt *exhilarated*.

She stared out the window at the sand dunes of the planet below. Zerzura. The legendary planet packed with danger, mystery and history.

She was *finally* here. All she could see was sand dune, after yellow sand dune, all the way off into the distance. The dual suns hung in the sky, big and full—one gold and one red—baking the ground below.

But there was more to Zerzura than that. She knew, from all her extensive history training as an astro-archeologist, that the planet was covered in ruins—some old and others beyond ancient. She knew every single one of the myths and legends.

She glanced down at her lap and clutched the Sync communicator she was holding. Right here she had her ticket to finding an ancient Terran treasure.

Lexa thumbed the screen. She'd found the slim, ancient vase in the museum archives and initially thought nothing of the lovely etchings of priestesses on the side of it.

Until she'd finished translating the obscure text.

She'd been gobsmacked when she realized the text gave her clues that not only formed a map, but also described what the treasure was at the end. A famed Fabergé egg.

Excitement zapped like electricity through her veins. After a career spent mostly in the Galactic Institute of Historical Preservation and on a few boring digs in the central systems, she was now the curator of the Darend Museum on Zeta Volantis—a private and well-funded museum that was mostly just a place for her wealthy patron, Marius Darend, to house his extensive, private collection of invaluable artifacts from around the galaxy.

But like most in the galaxy, he had a special obsession with old Earth artifacts. When she'd gone to him with the map and proposal to go on a treasure hunt to Zerzura to recover it, he'd been more than happy to fund it.

So here she was, Dr. Alexa Carter, on a treasure hunt.

Her father, of course, had almost had a coronary when she'd told her parents she'd be gone for several weeks. That familiar hard feeling invaded her belly. Baron Carter did not like his only daughter working, let alone being an astro-archeologist, and he *really* didn't like her going to a planet like Zerzura. He'd ranted about wild chases and wastes of time, and predicted her failure.

She straightened in her seat. She'd been ignoring her father's disapproval for years. When she had the egg in her hands, then he'd have to swallow his words.

Someone leaned over her, a broad shoulder brushing hers. "Strap in, Princess, we're about to land."

Lexa's excitement deflated a little. There was just one fly in her med gel.

Unfortunately, Marius had insisted she bring along the museum's new head of security. She didn't know much about Damon Malik, but she knew she didn't like him. The rumor among the museum staff was that he had a super-secret military background.

She looked at him now, all long, and lean and dark. He had hair as black as her own, but skin far darker. She couldn't see him in the military. His manner was too... well, she wasn't sure what, exactly, but he certainly didn't seem the type to happily take orders.

No, he preferred to be the one giving them.

He shot her a small smile, but it didn't reach his dark eyes. Those midnight-blue eyes were always...intense. Piercing. Like he was assessing everything, calculating. She found it unsettling.

"I'm already strapped in, Mr. Malik." She tugged on her harness and raised a brow.

"Just checking. I'm here to make sure you don't get hurt on this little escapade."

"Escapade?" She bit her tongue and counted to ten. "We have a map leading to the location of a very valuable artifact. That's hardly an escapade."

"Whatever helps you sleep at night, Princess." He shot a glance at the window and the unforgiving desert below. "This is a foolish risk for some silly egg."

She huffed out a breath. Infuriating man. "Why get a job at a museum if you think artifacts are silly?"

He leaned back in his seat. "Because I needed a change. One where no one tried to kill me."

Kill him? She narrowed her eyes and wondered again just what the hell he'd done before he'd arrived at the Darend.

A chime sounded and the pilot's voice filtered into the plush cabin of Marius' starship. "Landing at Kharga spaceport in three minutes. Hang on, ladies and gentlemen."

Excitement filled Lexa's belly. Ignoring the man beside her, she looked out the window again.

The town of Kharga was visible now. They flew directly over it, and she marveled at the primitive look and the rough architecture. The buildings were made of stone—some simple squares, others with domed roofs, and some a haphazard sprawl of both. In the dirt-lined streets, ragged beasts were led by robed locals, and battered desert speeders flew in every direction, hovering off the ground.

It wasn't advanced and yes, it was rough and dangerous. So very different to the marble-lined floors and grandeur of the Darend Museum or the Institute's huge, imposing museums and research centers. And it was the complete opposite of the luxury she'd grown up with in the central systems.

She barely resisted bouncing in her seat like a child. She couldn't *wait* to get down there. She wasn't stupid, she knew there were risks, but could hold her own and she knew when to ask for help.

The ship touched down, a cloud of dust puffing past the window. Lexa ripped her harness off, trying—and failing—to contain her excitement.

"Wait." Damon grabbed her arm and pulled her back from the opening door. "I'll go first."

As he moved forward, she pulled a face at his broad back. *Arrogant know-it-all.*

The door opened with a quiet hiss. She watched him stop at the top of the three steps that had extended from the starship. He scanned the spaceport...well, spaceport was a generous word for it. Lexa wasn't sure the sandy ground, beaten-up starships lined up beside them, and the battered buildings covered with black streaks—were those laser scorch marks?—warranted the term spaceport, but it was what it was.

Damon checked the laser pistols holstered at his lean hips then nodded. "All right." He headed down the steps.

Lexa tugged on the white shirt tucked into her fitted khaki pants. Mr. Dark and Brooding might be dressed in all black, but she'd finally pulled her rarely used expedition clothes out of her closet for the trip. She couldn't wait to get them dirty. She tucked her Sync into her small backpack, swung the bag over her shoulder and headed down the stairs.

"Our contact is supposed to meet us here." She looked around but didn't see anyone paying them much attention. A rough-looking freighter crew lounged near a starfreighter that didn't even look like it could make it off the ground. A couple of robed humanoids argued with three smaller-statured reptilians. "He's a local treasure hunter called Brocken Phoenix."

Damon grunted. "Looks like he's late. I suggest we head to the central market and ask around."

"Okay." She was eager to see more of Kharga and soak it all in.

"Stay close to me."

Did he have to use that autocratic tone all the time? She tossed him a salute.

Something moved through his dark eyes before he shook his head and started off down the dusty street.

As they neared the market, the crowds thickened. The noise increased as well. People had set up makeshift stalls, tables, and tents and were selling...well, just about everything.

There was a hawker calling out the features of his droids. Lexa raised a brow. The array available was interesting—from stocky maintenance droids to life-like syndroids made to look like humans. Other sellers were offering clothes, food, weapons, collectibles, even dragon bones.

Then she saw the cages.

She gasped. "Slavers."

Damon looked over and his face hardened. "Yeah."

The first cage held men. All tall and well-built. Laborers. The second held women. Anger shot through her. "It can't be legal."

"We're a long way from the central systems, Princess. You'll find lots of stuff here on Zerzura that isn't legal."

"We have to—"

He raised a lazy brow. "Do something? Unless you've got a whole bunch of e-creds I don't know about or an army in your back pocket, there isn't much we can do."

Her stomach turned over and she looked away. He might be right, but did he have to be so cold about it?

"Look." He pointed deeper into the market at a dusty, domed building with a glowing neon sign above the door. "That bar is where I hear the treasure hunters gather."

She wondered how he'd heard anything about the place when they'd only been dirtside a few minutes. But she followed him toward the bar, casting one last glance at the slaves.

As they neared the building, a body flew outward through the arched doorway. The man hit the dirt, groaning. He tried to stand before flopping face first back into the sand.

Even from where they stood, Lexa smelled the liquor fumes wafting off him. Nothing smooth and sweet like what was available back on Zeta Volantis. No, this smelled like homebrewed rotgut.

Damon stepped over the man with barely a glance. At the bar entrance, he paused. "I think you should stay out here. It'll be safer. I'll find out what I can about Phoenix and be right back."

She wanted to argue, but right then, two huge giants slammed out of the bar, wrestling each other. One was an enormous man, almost seven feet tall, with some aquatic heritage. He had pale-blue skin, large, wide-set eyes and tiny gills on the side of his neck. His opponent was human with a mass of dreadlocked brown hair, who stood almost as tall and broad.

The human slammed a giant fist into the aquatic's face, shouting in a language Lexa's lingual implant didn't recognize. That's when Lexa realized the dreadlocked man was actually a woman.

A security droid floated out of the bar. Its laser

weapons swiveled to aim at the fighting pair. "You are no longer welcome at the Desert Dragon. Please vacate the premises."

Grumbling, the fighters pulled apart, then shuffled off down the street.

Lexa swallowed. "Fine. I'll stay out here."

"Stay close," Damon warned.

She tossed him another mock salute and when he scowled, she felt a savage sense of satisfaction. Then he turned and ducked inside.

She turned back to study the street. One building down, she saw a stall holder standing behind a table covered in what looked like small artifacts. Lexa's heart thumped. She had to take a look.

"All original. Found here on Zerzura." The older man spread his arms out over his wares. "Very, very old." His eyes glowed in his ageless face topped by salt-and-pepper hair. "Very valuable."

"May I?" Lexa indicated a small, weathered statue.

The man nodded. "But you break, you buy."

Lexa studied the small figurine. It was supposed to resemble a Terran fertility statue—a woman with generous hips and breasts. She tested the weight of it before she sniffed and set it down. "It's not a very good fake. I'd say you create a wire mesh frame, set it in a mold, then pour a synthetic plas in. You finish it off by spraying it with some sort of rock texture."

The man's mouth slid into a frown.

Lexa studied the other items. Jewelry, small boxes and inscribed stones. She fingered a necklace. It was by no means old but it was pretty.

Then she spotted it.

A small, red egg, covered in gold-metalwork and resting on a little stand.

She picked it up, cradling its slight weight. The craftwork was terrible but there was no doubt it was a replica of a Fabergé egg.

"What is this?" she asked the man.

He shrugged. "Lots of myths about the Orphic Priestesses around here. They lived over a thousand years ago and the egg was their symbol."

Lexa stroked the egg.

The man's keen eyes narrowed in on her. "It's a pretty piece. Said to be made in the image of the priestesses' most valuable treasure, the Goddess Egg. It was covered in Terran rubies and gold."

A basic history. Lexa knew from her research that the Goddess Egg had been brought to Zerzura by Terran colonists escaping the Terran war and had been made by a famed jeweler on Earth named Fabergé. Unfortunately, most of its history had been lost.

Someone bumped into Lexa from behind. She ignored it, shifting closer to the table.

Then a hard hand clamped down on her elbow and jerked her backward. The little red egg fell into the sand.

Lexa expected the cranky stall owner to squawk about the egg and demand payment. Instead, he scampered backward with wide eyes and turned away.

Lexa's accoster jerked her around.

"Hey," she exclaimed.

Then she looked up. Way up.

The man was part-reptilian, with iridescent scales

covering his enormous frame. He stood somewhere over six and a half feet with a tough face that looked squashed.

"Let me go." She slapped at his hand. *Idiot.*

He was startled for a second and did release her. Then he scowled, which turned his face from frightening to terrifying. "Give me your e-creds." He grabbed her arm, large fingers biting into her flesh, and shook her. "I want everything transferred to my account."

Lexa raised a brow. "Or what?"

With his other hand, he withdrew a knife the length of her forearm. "Or I use this."

The Phoenix Adventures

Among Galactic Ruins
At Star's End
In the Devil's Nebula
On a Rogue Planet
Beneath a Trojan Moon
Beyond Galaxy's Edge
On a Cyborg Planet
Return to Dark Earth
On a Barbarian World
Lost in Barbarian Space
Through Uncharted Space

ALSO BY ANNA HACKETT

Treasure Hunter Security

Undiscovered

Uncharted

Unexplored

Unfathomed

Untraveled

Unmapped

Galactic Gladiators

Gladiator

Warrior

Hero

Protector

Champion

Barbarian

Beast

Rogue

Guardian

Cyborg

Also Available as Audiobooks!

Hell Squad

Marcus

Cruz

Gabe

Reed

Roth

Noah

Shaw

Holmes

Niko

Finn

Theron

Hemi

Ash

Levi

Manu

Also Available as Audiobooks!

The Anomaly Series

Time Thief

Mind Raider

Soul Stealer

Salvation

Anomaly Series Box Set

The Phoenix Adventures

Among Galactic Ruins

At Star's End

In the Devil's Nebula

On a Rogue Planet

Beneath a Trojan Moon

Beyond Galaxy's Edge

On a Cyborg Planet

Return to Dark Earth

On a Barbarian World

Lost in Barbarian Space

Through Uncharted Space

Crashed on an Ice World

Perma Series

Winter Fusion

A Galactic Holiday

Warriors of the Wind

Tempest

Storm & Seduction

Fury & Darkness

Standalone Titles

Savage Dragon

Hunter's Surrender

One Night with the Wolf

For more information visit AnnaHackettBooks.com

I'm a USA Today bestselling author and I'm passionate about ***action romance***. I love stories that combine the thrill of falling in love with the excitement of action, danger and adventure. I'm a sucker for that moment when the team is walking in slow motion, shoulder-to-shoulder heading off into battle. I write about people overcoming unbeatable odds and achieving seemingly impossible goals. I like to believe it's possible for all of us to do the same.

My books are mixture of action, adventure and sexy romance and they're recommended for anyone who enjoys fast-paced stories where the boy wins the girl at the end (or sometimes the girl wins the boy!)

For release dates, action romance info, free books, and other fun stuff, sign up for the latest news here:

Website: www.annahackettbooks.com

Printed in Great Britain
by Amazon